GOODBYE, AGAIN

GOODBYE, AGAIN

Richard Klayman

Bassett Books
Bassett, Virginia

Goodbye, Again

Library of Congress Cataloging in Publication Data
Klayman, Richard.
        Goodbye, Again.

Ethnic Relations
93-71889

ISBN 0-9632415-2-4

Chapter One

Mystic, Massachusetts

"The world may come to know our prayers, but it will never know our pain." The rabbi's words came not from the crumbled paper that he dangled between his long, white fingers but from his heart. He was an old man, old before he came to America, one of the desperate generations that passed out of Russia and Poland, bringing all that was Yiddish to America. Now, the rabbi was ancient. His humped back sat upon a tall, bony frame. He was clean shaven, never having adopted a beard, his single capitulation to a modernity that was hopelessly outdistanced by the passion of his faith. Without the aid of glasses, his steel-blue eyes spanned across the rolling landscape of burial stones. He did not strain to see whatever was before him. He merely accepted what it was his eyes witnessed.

Despite his years of providing spiritual comfort, the rabbi was shaken. This passing, this death, confused him. He had difficulty administering comfort and perspective, and, reluctant as he might be to admit it, he balked at giving that human resignation before the Lord's will.

The rabbi's words, "our prayers...our pain," had symmetry to them, and they disguised as much as they foretold. "Who listens to our prayers; who knows our pain?"

Perhaps the rabbi felt a bit lost. After all, he would be the first to admit that he was a solitary figure. There was pain in his calling, that was a reality of the profession. Still, the rabbi believed that all prayers find a place of ultimate rest. Yet his faith tugged at his anger. Maybe it was folly to stammer at his finiteness in a world full of mysteries and silence, but the rabbi's heart grieved.

Standing on the summer hillside, clothed in a dark suit, the rabbi's presence stood out from the green and yellow grasses. He appeared odd or somehow quite alien from the surroundings of sunbaked earth, an endless blue sky, and the air that nearly sucked breath out of his body. Here he was, conducting a ceremony over five thousand years in the making, five thousand years of struggle. And though this hillside was in New England, the relevance of prayers like the quest for some meaning to life required a constant battling. Here he was giving a eulogy, but, as with each goodbye, there was a message of hope. Even America needs hope, the old man thought. And he then whispered under a sigh, "Death. Hope. America." For an immigrant rabbi addressing an audience of first and second generation Jews, there was something quite unfathomable about a suicide in America. "Our prayers...our pain," the words reverberated in the rabbi's mind.

Weren't the words the essence of all who hoped that America offered a listening ear to prayers and a respite from the suffering? All who were dispossessed, all who sought sanctuary in America, looked to America for an answer. No wonder that each newcomer's suitcase was remarkably alike, fastened by straps of expectation and filled with memories. And there were fears, too, including the fear that America ignored their language, enticed their children, contorted their religion, and minimized their identity. America gave; America took. This was the nature of the bargain.

The wrinkles that covered the old man's neck made his pink skin stand out, sculpture-like, from the black tie and white shirt that draped his body. He ran his hand down a side of his face. A breeze fanned the stubby grass.

****

His firm voice and emotional words were heard with an unsuspected attentiveness by a spectator. A man set himself off from the funeral party. The rabbi spied him but paid little attention to his presence. Jake Newman sat atop a sloping hillside by a small dedication marker announcing that this was the Cemetery of Congregation Beth Israel, Established 1878.

When Newman was a child, it was this hillside that had provided him a secluded spot from which to watch the world. Now in 1941, nearly three decades later, his first moments back to the town of his birth found him on the same nurturing piece of land, observing the funeral of the one individual who had made Mystic important to him.

None of this was lost on Newman, and he was moved by the words of the rabbi. The rabbi's words and the ancient Hebrew chants that brought peace to the grave-side scene impressed Newman. He was no stranger to the life of a small Jewish community, a Jewish shtetl. He felt the sun on his hands. The Hebrew prayers filled the air with a low, mournful plea. Newman closed his eyes, and he could sense this place, a place he once called home. In fact, it was that shtetl existence that had prompted him to walk away from a life that had squeezed at him and would have, he felt, denied him the full fruits of the earth. Newman was not one to live a life in study or in prayer. The sun that warmed his hands had always stirred his mind. The sun, the sea, and everything in between was Newman's delight. "You are a strange one," one of his public school teachers had remarked. "A Jewish Huck Finn ... is that what you are?"

****

The mourners listened, their faces acknowledging the rabbi's prayers as part of their special heritage. Jewish life made them recognize and accept a certain otherness about themselves. As Jews, they lived according to a different calendar. They were part of a tribe different from that of their neighbors. Death confirmed the frailty of an unmistakable separateness of that life.

Most of the funeral party had followed the well laid out paths. Others darted between gravestones, making paths of their own. The gravestones acted as signposts. After a slight touching of the granite, the mourners found the next step. Cool to the hands, the gravestones provided balance and respite before the sight of the newly-dug grave. The oppressive July air denied the relief the usual sea breezes provided the cities and towns north of Boston. Reprieve could come only in the evening if a strong sea breeze made its way inland or, God willing, a shift in the wind summoned dry air. New England's weather was so unpredictable; its gyrations were followed with as much interest and obsession as was the game of summer, baseball.

Now standing over the grave, the rabbi continued his service. In Hebrew and then in English, his prayers exalted the dust whence we come and where we return. "Who can doubt the majesty and the omnipotence of God?"

"But the pain," the rabbi lamented, "is all that this family and community can endure. The pain is ours alone. God's ways are not clear to us humble mortals tested to the limits of our frailties, yet remaining God fearing and God loving." Speaking in a low voice, the old man questioned, "Is not this our place, our purpose? Is this journey too much for our spirits? Are we to be punished for faltering spirits, dear God? Jenny Glass was a young woman, young with hopes and convictions, but as wise as any person as to the need for justice and peace for every person. Her end troubles me; her end tortures me. Were we asked to understand the ravages of plague and disease, this we could at least fathom and, doubtless, accept. But the illness of the mind, nay, the illness of the spirit, this is too much for our hearts. Dust we are, but why God? Why does your wisdom rip our hearts today? Helpless as in the darkest night, extinguished with but a flicker, still are we not worthy of some warning, some sign that might make us prepared for your will? Is this the method to remind us of your wondrous power and that we are to bend before your will? Have mercy on us, have mercy on our children. Our devotion may be less than you desire, but it remains our ultimate purpose. Believe us, our God, believe us that your commandments are supreme."

"But, of course, God does not answer us, does not consult us about His grand design, does not confer with us as to the timing or even the circumstances of His decisions. Ha-Shem, the ever- living spirit of spirits, guide us in accepting your ways."

The old man opened a black prayer book and proceeded to chant and quite simply to cry. His voice made the Hebrew prayers conform to the swaying grass and tree branches caught up in the hot winds.

The most immediate members of the family made their way by the casket now descending into the ground, every passer-by taking a shovel of soil and filling in the space between the ground and the unstained and knotted pine box. A last sprinkle of earth upon the casket, a final chant, and the service finished.

****

Out of immediate sight were three gravediggers. They sat on the dried out grass waiting for all to leave so that they might begin their job of filling in the grave, setting a marker of twine on small sticks all about the site, and tidying the ground to make it seem that neither spade nor shovel engaged in anything as sobering as a funeral. And then all would be quiet. Finally, the earth and the air could sigh a relief that they could be alone, and the dust would do its work, and the gravediggers could go about their own lives.

Newman lingered by the grave site in no hurry to move

on. He circled the grave and meandered through the rows of nearby tombstones with an ease and dispassion that mourners in a cemetery do not ordinarily display. All the while, the cemetery workers proceeded with their work, anxious to get the hot summer's work behind them.

Jake Newman was a lanky man. His short, yellow hair came to a widow's peak, and his skin had been burnt by the elements. Although his limbs were thin and long, he was quite strong and obviously fit, as though his work had conditioned him or demanded too much in the way of his energies. He sat on the grass watching the cemetery workers bring down the tent and fold up the graveside walkways and roped off dividers that led to the grave site.

Before their job was finished, Newman walked over to them. Sweating and hurrying, a white- haired man and a short, dark-haired man, both shirtless, worked with long-handled shovels while a young Black man tore into the dried pile of earth with a pick.

"Big funeral for a hot day," Newman offered. He took a blue handkerchief from his back pocket and wiped his neck and his face. He noticed a jug of water nearby, but the laborers did not offer him a drink. All three men showed the signs of their labors and were pleased to stop the work. The older white men grabbed some shade from one of the larger gravestones, while the young Black fellow headed for a spot behind a stone a bit away from his co-workers.

"Yeah, a woman about fifty, I was told. She took enough of those damn sleeping pills to kill five people ... that's the way I heard it. You part of the crowd here?" the older fellow asked, his shovel tamping down the earth, smoothing a bump and filling in a crevice.

"Yes, I guess I am. Jenny Glass, the woman, she was forty-four years old," Newman interjected. "Don't mean to hold you fellows up."

Clearly the job of filling in the grave had stopped, conversation being more agreeable than working in the heat. It was too hot to rush.

Newman sensed the gravediggers' willingness to lean on their tools, and he continued. "Visiting in a way. I lived around here a ways back. Just a little visit, just a little business, too. I spent a lot of time on this hill, a lot of time on most of the hills all around here. The only thing that's changed is the cemetery which is getting full." A tired laugh drifted out of the two men.

Newman gave a short, military salute goodbye, but before he could go, the dark-haired fellow spoke to him.

"I remember you," he said.

Despite the passage of many years, a small town remains the same, and the links of people to the ebb and flow of the town remains in one memory or another. Newman looked into the fellow's face, and he remembered the contours of the face although he did not recall the fellow's name nor could he place him as a brother or sister of somebody equally elusive.

"Sure," Newman lied.

But later, after Newman had departed, the gravedigger would tell his companions, "His name was Newman. He was a Suffolk Square guy. My family lived near his house, a three-decker near the town line."

The gravedigger continued with a touch of harshness. "Haughty, haughty as hell. He'd let you know what was on his mind. Remember Ralph - Ralph DeVisone; there was a guy who was into everything - booze, guns, you name it. Jesus, was he one onery dude. Anyway, he said to that Newman guy, maybe there was some kind of argument between the two of them or something like that, `What you looking at, Newman?' Yeah, I remember. It was after Newman found out old Ralph had offered a reward, a bounty on his head, for anybody who would beat the hell out of him.

`What you looking at, Newman?' Ralph says.

"Newman doesn't bat an eye and says, `I'm looking at a real piece of crap!' Just like that. To old Ralph. Ralph almost blew the eyes out of his head, but all he says to Newman is, `Man, you are playing with fire. One of these days you're going to get burned!'"

The young Black man, listening, questioned the gravedigger. "What about the reward? Who got the reward money?"

"Jesus. What's with you? Nobody got the reward. Nobody wanted to fool with that guy. He was like the weather - just when you'd think everything was calm, mother nature bites you in the rear. Newman lived on the edge of town, right by the marshes; it was nothing but swamps at the time. Now there are houses and streets and all kinds of shit, but once they was nothing but marsh weeds. The highest cottontails grew eight or nine feet tall, and the damn tides poured in from the ocean."

"When I say Newman lived on the swamps, I ain't foolin' ya. He was one weird kid who used to spend his time floating on pounded-down oil tanks. Made 'em into rafts, and he knew those damn swamps like they was his backyard. Go into those swamps and you'd meet up with him. He was like some swamp rat. I knew a kid who found hisself almost drowned in that place. He was one Hebe who'd other Hebes stayed away from."

****

The weather was cooling down, but Newman stopped his walk to take off his coat and roll up his sleeves anyway. On his right forearm was a large blue gash, at least a quarter-inch wide, that travelled up beyond his shirt and up to the top of his shoulder. Newman stared at it as he rolled up his shirt sleeves.

It was hard for him to believe that thirty years had gone by since he had run off to join the United States Merchant Marines. Every time he saw that scar his mind wandered to the merchant marines, the ships and the sea, and what seemed like a life that belonged to him but had disappeared from the life that he now led. Of course, one of the parts of that life was the fact that it was here, in the town of Mystic, that all of that having to do with the ships and the sea had its beginning. It seemed as though that was all so long ago, so long that he tried to resist unfurling all the years and the dates and all the baggage of the past.

Still he had spent his youth here. The son of an orthodox Jewish man, he had been hungry for a life of travel, for the outdoors, for everything from sea birds to the railroad tracks. Ironic, he thought, his father now was dead, but here he was back in the place that he had been so eager to leave. No one knew more of its nooks, winding roads, meadows and paths than Newman. He remembered the streets lined with three-decker tenements which fanned out from Suffolk Square. All of the paths and alleys and all of the fields in between were well understood by him, used by him as he navigated through them by day or night.

Butcher shops, tailors, and small grocery stores dotted the two main intersections of the Square. On street corners, young men would station themselves, gaining a place in the sun that many kept for a lifetime. After all, if making a living meant continuing to live in one apartment or another, the street corner took on the identity of another room in the apartment. Even in the rain, the locals could be found huddled under an overhang waiting for the weather to change or passing the time saying hello to passersby, bantering with the shopkeepers or gossiping with friends. Their conversation was filled with ideas about the making and selling of just about anything, bragging about positions just beyond the horizon. "I know a man who became a millionaire selling shoelaces. Shoelaces! Don't you believe me?" So went the discussions.

In Mystic the cafeterias were for those too tired to prepare their food or too in need of conversation to be satisfied with food alone. The next generation needed to get a sense that young adulthood promised better things ahead. In the meantime, they pulled up a piece of stone or brick wall, waiting for the call of America that work needed to be done with speed and for profit.

Newman noticed that a delicatessen had taken root on one of the corners of Suffolk Square; but, try as he might, Newman could not remember the restaurant or what had preceded it. He took one step from the sidewalk to the entranceway of the restaurant and pushed the screen door inward. Red, gingham tablecloths covered the small square tables that lined the windowed half of the store with a half dozen other tables scattered about. A glass-covered meat case displayed salami, desserts, and side dishes of potato salad, pickles, and vegetables. Barrels nearby breathed of garlic. Newman picked up the wooden cover of one of them and found it full of green tomatoes amid spices, cloves of garlic, and a brine that filled the barrel to within three inches from the top.

He sat at a table near the window and watched the passing flow of shoppers: old men with shirts open at the collar, women dressed in shifts, and children holding hands with an adult. A man in a white apron and a short-sleeved white shirt came to his table.

"What can I get you?" he asked.

Newman turned his neck toward the counter and noticed another fellow cutting some kind of meat.

"What's he cutting there?"

"Murray, is that the brisket?"

Even before the answer, "brisket", came back the room became crowded as three groups of men walked in, filling up the tables and straining to get a look at the glass, food cases.

"That will be fine," Newman said. "However you do it is fine, but not a sandwich. A platter with black coffee, please. Could I have the coffee now?"

Everything about the place made Newman remember things that he had not actually forgotten but had placed aside in his mind and his heart. Now he forced himself to recall why it was that these smells of the restaurant and the people eating and talking in the place jostled his being. He sensed a closeness to these strangers that reminded him of his family and his childhood. Newman looked up as his food was brought to him. Besides his brisket, the plate contained tsimmes, a combination of carrots and sweet potato, that covered the entire plate.

Chapter Two

Jenny's Song

What was it that she had written him? Newman's thoughts returned to Jenny. Was it in the last letter he had received from her? Yes, that was the last time. "This is my senior year. While you've been drifting about on your ships, I've all but finished here. My degree is about a month away. Don't ask me if it's been worth it. Yes, that is what you'd likely say."

"You would say that Yankee colleges have no great love for Jews who live in triple-decker tenements. You would say that the word `merit' is a battlefield casualty in Massachusetts ... maybe in all America!"

"You don't fool me Jake Newman. I know the kind of character you are, stowing away on your ships, making getaways from place to place. You're a sad sailor ... that is what I think of you. You have no faith in people, but I do. Ideas matter to me and to others, too. You don't trust anybody. I know, you'd say `a schmuck who went to college is only an educated schmuck.' Even your jokes don't fool me. You are a sad and lonely sailor."

"You would say, `Why aren't there more Blacks at the college? Why aren't there more Italians or Greeks or anybody else except for those who own the road?'"

"That is what you'd say, 'Who owns the road?'"

"If you must know, there are more and more of all kinds of people here. And it was worth it, at least for me. There was culture here. I don't mind saying that I've enjoyed it here. My classmates, the professors, and just the beauty of this little spot. I belonged here. I may have even more than belonged! Between the acting workshops and the dramas that I got a chance to work on ... well, it was the world I wanted to be a part of. So many of these people are brilliant. Yes, I know you hate that word, but they are. They're talented and have enormous knowledge about art and poetry, and I respect them. You are laughing, aren't you? Go ahead. I don't care."

You are a sad and lonely sailor,
Sailing on ships and seas.
You think that there is safety,
You think that you are free.

There is peace upon the water,
And comfort under the sky.
Nature's full of wonder,
In your heart and your eyes.

But you're still a sad and lonely fellow,
Who has taken to ships and seas.
I hope the waves protect you,
I pray the skies delight you.
I shall not fight you, if that's
your way to be.

But you can never fool me.
You can pretend to not hear,
How that sad and lonely sailor,
Pretends not to care.

You're a sad and lonely sailor,
You sail on ships and seas.
All the earth is full of lovers.
All the world settles for a home.
You'd rather not believe, you'd rather
be free to flee.

You are a sad and lonely sailor,
Out of reach to hear my song.
A sad and lonely sailor,
Happy to be gone.

Those were Jenny's last words to him. For at least a few years, he had thought of them, and he thought about her song many times.

****

After graduation from Middlesex College, Jenny began working in its library. As a child she had loved books and had never grown bored, doubtful, or contemptuous of them. Her job gave her an opportunity to go about her work with a degree of freedom. She conducted library research for the faculty, frequently finding herself fascinated by the subjects they were engaged in researching. Two hours a day she maintained her vigil at the front desk, checking in or out the afternoon books. Since the winter afternoons were not busy, she had time to review the latest acquisitions. Travel books and poetry were her favorites. Jenny liked to think of herself as a poetess, though this image was something she never talked about. Her love of writing belonged to a side of her that few even realized existed.

For a while many of her classmates lived in Boston or Cambridge, and Jenny lived a rather Bohemian existence. She had her crowd. There were productions of one playwright or another; there were poetry readings; there were art exhibits that she loved; and there were trips to one New England spot or another for vacations or just to get away.

She had admirers, too. But they were usually part of a particular theatrical production, or a friend of a friend.

As the years went on, her crowd became smaller and more dispersed; finally she was alone. Oh, she had an extensive correspondence with this roommate or that old friend, but soon the college years gave way to the family years.

Poetry gave way to teaching for some, to business careers for others. Drama gave way to the drama of the courtroom or the boardroom or, simply, the comfortable club

17

that the family's name could all but guarantee. Eventually, the crowd vanished.

****

Outside of the library, Jenny loved to ride her bicycle. How grand, she thought, to be so enthralled with a sport that little else mattered. The streets of Cambridge and the bends of the Charles River were well-known to her. Sometimes she wished to be anonymous, but sometimes, especially on the weekends, she'd stop at one of the coffee shops to wave at people who had grown so familiar to her that they were near-ly friends. Since a bicyclist is expected to survey the road ahead, she had the perfect opportunity to keep her head up and drink in the landscape until she was satiated.

She had ridden bikes her entire life. Though self-taught, she had clearly perfected her skill, and that was part of her love for riding, too. Of course, having someone to ride with her could be fun, she reflected; then again a partner might get in the way. After work, she'd ride her bike down the three-mile stretch of road to her home, a rented half of an old colonial house.

Her apartment was hidden from the casual observer. Directly to the rear of the house was a street-level entrance-way. A narrow stairway led to Jenny's place. A large kitchen and three smaller rooms made up the apartment. Below the stairs was a place for her bike and a few pieces of furniture she had not decided to keep or discard. A two-seat, white wicker sofa provided a nook for her to nap on or cozy up to read.

What was special about the house was Carl Harland, its owner and occupant. Carl was a retired schoolteacher who had lived in the town for fifty years and who loved having Jenny rent his place. "You're the kind of tenant I want," she remembered him telling her. "I can't stand renting to men because there's always the likelihood of a problem. Usually it's liquor. If not, then it's women, and then the neighbors let me know. Someone quiet and dependable - that's what I want. I go about my business and that's the way I like it. My family and I do not like change."

Harland's family was two Boston terriers and two Siamese cats. The cats, Spud and Cleo, were as adorable as they were perverse. Their howls and crying could be prevented only by Mr. Harland's or Jenny's warm lap. The bulging-eyed terriers, George and Gracey, were as demanding as the cats. "But," thought Jenny, "I do love them - odd as they and their eccentric master may be."

At night, Jenny found opening the door to her apartment an adventure although nothing changed in her life, not really changed. She rarely had guests, and she rarely wanted any. She wanted her home to be a refuge. When her work at the library was through, her commitment to the wider world was over. She wanted the kind of peace that people only talked about - complete uninvolvement. With the door closed, Jenny could feel relief that the day was over and that she had made it back to her house. Sometimes one or both of the cats greeted her, but, thankfully, they were not her responsibility.

Jenny's mother, Frances, lived in Mystic. They saw one another only on family occasions or on Jewish holidays when they both worked hard to avoid a quarrel about the differences bottled up inside themselves. This restraint was a feat. Both mother and daughter were expressive, but they had tact when dealing with one another. Frances' sister, Gerdie, who did not share their reserve, often told Frances that Jenny expected her mother to help her get married or at least arrange a date for her.

Privately, Gerdie would think, "It's not normal for Jenny or her mother to let life go by without a family or a chance for a fuller life. Thank God," she would continue, "my Rachael has a family. And my Bernie, crazy as he is, still he has a family, a home. I can talk to him. He won't listen, but he has a family."

Sometimes Gerdie would become frantic with her sister's lack of planning. "Tell her, Frances. Tell her to get married. Frances, you are acting like a schmuck with her. She's not a spring chicken, you know. Everyone is getting older."

Though she did not let anyone know, Frances was as concerned as her sister. Her seeming indifference was the mask she wore because she understood her daughter. Jenny was not to be pushed. She had always been reclusive, always in need of the firmness that neither she nor her husband - may he rest in peace - could not or would not exert.

Leonard Glass had had his factory that had been a world within itself. His time had been the factory's. Little had he known what a small amount of time that would be. Dead for seven years now, Lennie had left Frances with only her Jenny. Although she knew her daughter's future could not be left to chance, she was unwilling to risk a misunderstanding that would rip Jenny from her and leave her alone. "Feuds and misunderstandings ravage too many families. I won't allow division to happen between Jenny and me. That she doesn't need. What she needs, may God in his wisdom tell her. The Lord does not need me to perform His work."

Frances' leg was heavily swollen. Having been to many doctors and tried as many remedies for its treatment, Frances rarely ventured out now and almost never visited her daughter.

"Anyway," Frances often thought, "marriage may not solve anything. I dare not say this out loud, but Jenny needs to get away from this place and her job. Jenny needs to be appreciated. Appreciated," Frances thought, "for being the beautiful flower she is." Frances faltered for a moment. "Appreciation. Where does one go for that?" she wondered. This made her perplexed and sad, though she said nothing.

Whether Jenny thought about Jake Newman or not, she rarely mentioned him to her mother. At college she had dated boys from her own school as well as from B.U., MIT, and Harvard. Although these dates were pleasant, Jenny

20

felt that her identity was submerged even though she talked freely about the arts, theatre, literature, and her interests. However, the man's career was always the important under-current to discussions about the future. Natural as this was, Jenny often thought that such discussions made her and her dreams less than a priority.

A mathematics major at MIT, whom she had dated a num-ber of times, had been eager for her to understand his future as a scientist. He was a man who would be sought after by major corporations, all of whom could promise him, and her, too, a life of financial rewards. In all of her conversations with this man, it was the prestige of "the Institute" that came through. Implied was the need to tailor their life to his profession - a profession that would turn the even most spon-taneous young man into a mask of what he would inevitably become.

Jenny's suitors shared none of her dreams, and she failed to be fascinated by their dreams. She especially rejected the idea of having to seek the approval from "the firm" or "the bank" or some other enterprise. Jenny may not have known or understood what her life was to be, but she was clear that an occupation would provide little in the way of a mission.

College made Jenny think of her life as an opportunity to make her world not only civil but harmonious. What was life without a credible vision of harmony with one's self? Jenny felt and hoped that life was not finished with introducing her to people and ideas that would build strength within her. Jenny's love of the world was unconditional, but her vision of reality, securely fixed as it was, could be outdistanced by her dreams. Such was her power and her frailty.

Jenny's father, Leonard, had been a first generation Jew in the town, not because of his birth but because he had lived there for thirty years. When Leonard was six, he and his father had left a small village outside of Kiev to come to America. In fact, he had never known his mother who had died in the "old country". Two years after coming to Mystic,

Lennie's father married a woman named Rose, and they had had two children: Morris and Celia. Lennie's stepmother treated him with love but with an icy detachment that neither she nor her stepson fully understood. Perhaps such aloofness, and frankly coldness, had made Lennie interested in facts. He believed that nuance was a hoax on the world, a crutch that motivated only those individuals looking for excuses.

"Getting through life successfully," Jenny recalled her father solemnly declare, "is a matter of putting money in the bank. Only then can taking money out of the bank be possible."

Perhaps these observations were the reason why Jenny had so detested banks. Her father portrayed banks as oracles for making sense of the world. "A bank is an impartial institution," he would tell her. "Banks need not supply leadership to the world, for inertia itself will lead. Banks only need to say yes or no."

Jenny would sigh. After all, her father was a nice man but helplessly in league with American boosterism, a cheerleader for profits and economic growth. His death had left Jenny and her mother comfortable in their own home, with a sufficient amount of cash and one or two investments. All to what purpose - that was a question that neither Jenny nor her mother voiced. Survival was an end within itself; the purpose of life was another matter.

Anyway, neither cared about financial extravagance. Frances had lived on next-to-nothing out of necessity as a child and out of habit ever since. Her family had been large and poor. Jenny lived frugally, never envisioning herself cushioned in a world of goods. Odd as it was, Lennie could have revelled in periodic bouts of materialism, yet he fought off these temptations with more hard work. Exhaustion saved him money and killed him at the same time.

Maybe it was this family life that had made Jenny less concerned that some man would come along and take care of her. It wasn't financial security that Jenny dreamed about. Jenny was motivated by a sense of fitting in to a world that had meaning - a world of changing seasons, of poetry, and a world that emphasized belonging.

Lennie and Frances had done all that any parent could. They had established guideposts, but their guideposts did not lead to what mattered, at least not to Jenny. Neither her parents nor Jenny saw any sense in making a fuss about such personal differences, even had they noticed. What was to be gained?

****

Newman left the restaurant and walked around the Suffolk Square shopping area. A sidewalk repair crew was putting new curbstones on one part of the main road. Because of the heat, the men worked without shirts, and in slow but steady strides they went about their labors. He looked at their faces to see if any were familiar, but he quickly discovered that they were unknown to him. Nevertheless, he enjoyed watching them place stones of granite with precision. A calm, methodical quality set the pace of their work, a rhythm which evidenced understanding about not only the stone but the climate and the manner in which rock settles over time.

The Square itself was small, containing single-story shops that the predominantly orthodox Jewery of the neighborhood depended on for shopping. The creamery store remained in the center of the Square almost unchanged from what Newman recalled. Barrels of pickles were placed in front of one of the two large picture windows that looked into the aisles and upon the shelves of the store. Ice chests and cutting blocks displayed the same farmers cheese and fish that were there when his father had instructed him to pick up herring, smoked mackerel, sable, or other delights.

Today, after his meal, Newman was not in the mood to go

from store to store. Jenny's funeral continued to haunt his mind, unsettling him. A trolley heading for Boston pulled up in front of a small drugstore. Newman jumped on board. He tossed in a bunch of coins in the fare box which stood four feet high in front of the conductor. Going to an empty single seat near the rear of the car, Newman became one of a handful of passengers. Feeling himself intrigued and cramped by his memories and the physical smallness of the Square, he needed a few hours someplace, anyplace else. He sat and looked out the window of the trolley. His memories had their own way of demanding Newman's attention.

****

Fall 1927 ...

Newman's room at the Charlestown YMCA was a Spartan place, containing a bed with a heavy iron frame and a thin dresser with a twelve-inch mirror fastened on the opposite wall. From his bed, he could look out the window into the Charlestown Navy Yard. Old Ironsides, the revolutionary war but still commissioned frigate, sat in the harbor. Away from the water was the Bunker Hill Monument, peering from the heights of narrow cobblestone streets and brick-faced brownstones.

Charlestown was as Irish Catholic as Suffolk Square was Jewish. But Charlestown possessed a combination of pride and arrogance that scoffed at the outside world, particularly at the gentility which Boston had wrapped about itself. The hills and the row houses, the churches of stone, and the warehouses of clapboards were the trademarks of local life which could not be erased. The next generation of "Townies" adored all that had been there before them. Suffolk Square, on the other hand, never considered the next generation. Never was a marker laid; no commemoration of a building or an event or some other form of recognition was set aside.

Was that the difference between Charlestown and Suffolk Square? Was one generation's task to erase the life of the preceding generation? First-generation Jews expected their sons and daughters to succeed and thus exhausted themselves and their environment toward that end. Newman felt somewhat self-conscious about this.

At the foot of Prison Point Bridge, just as one approached Charlestown, was the famous Charlestown State Prison, the place that served its prisoners fried baloney three times a day and that had a wing set up for those notorious bank robbers and the most publicized of murderers. The prison boasted an electric chair. Newman had memories of what many viewed as a dreaded place. His father had served as a chaplain for the Jewish prisoners.

****

Jolted by the trolley, Newman stopped his reverie. "Pardon me. Could you tell me the time?" he asked the passenger in the seat in front of him.

Releasing her package to the floor, the dark- haired lady with tiny round-shaped glasses looked at her watch. "Five-thirty," she replied.

"Could it be?" Newman wondered. Losing track of time was one of the major shortcomings of working on land as opposed to a life at sea.

Even though the weather looked ominous, Newman had spent enough years in the Boston area to know that the weather would not reveal itself early in the morning. Newman saw a glimpse of sun dart between heavy clouds. The air was dry. Doubtless, some Canadian mass of cool air had forced itself down across the St. Lawrence River Valley and had made its way across New York state to fight off a low pressure system rising out of the South. This situation often occurred in New England. It was a natural way the air kept cool. Newman thought about the weather not for any special reason, but because it had such an influence upon his mood. Long ago, Newman had surmised a kind of sensitivity to the outdoors, or a simple feeling in sync with himself based on the kind of day that greeted him. It wasn't that he felt restricted by the clouds or the rain; it was just that his sense of himself, that dimension of his personality or identity would emerge or otherwise reflect itself, was shaped by the outside world. In determining what face to put on for the day, some folks were affected by other people. For Newman the weather at hand and the weather around the corner gave him his sense of how to master the pace of a day.

Again, the trolley rolled by the Charlestown YMCA. Newman recalled his room and the period of recuperation he experienced many years ago.

****

Fall, 1927 ...

A folded piece of paper had been slipped under his door. Lifting the enclosed half, he read the pencil scroll. "Where have you been? Looked for you all day, and my Ma wants to see you, too. Meet me at Duffy's Bar tonight about 9:00. See you then and don't forget. Jim."

Newman folded the paper and placed it in his wallet atop the dresser. It was an invitation that he would not be able to accept. As he turned, he caught a glimpse of himself in the mirror. His growth of overnight beard had darkened his already brown skin. At thirty-three years old, Newman had eyes that looked tired. His hair was so unkempt that for a minute he thought about combing it. Thinking that act would be hopeless, he ran a hand over his head instead. He felt a little skin on top of his head. "Am I going bald, too?" he worried.

A long, red scar stretched from a portion of his shoulder finally stopping along his right forearm. In the port of Jaffa he had side-swiped a young Jewish motorcyclist as he tried to evade a British patrol vehicle. The gangly rider was being chased because he had blown away part of a police station.

He was a dark-haired fellow no more than twenty years old. He looked exactly the way Mr. Simon told him he would look. "Simply back out your little Fiat into the lane and you will have done me a great service, Mr. Newman. The British will love the idea that an American sailor inadvertently botched the work of a terrorist. First impressions are full of pitfalls and are deceiving. In time the British authorities will realize their error, just as we expect them to do. The fellow you will stop will be anything but that. He is connected to the British, but he believes in our cause. Do you see what I mean?" the old man smiled a look of compassion.

"You want me to help get the British off the back of one fellow and onto the trail of someone else, someone who will be a dead end for them?" Newman surmised.

"Exactly. Exactly, Mr, Newman. That would be wonderful of you. Truly wonderful."

All went according to plan until the young motorcyclist grabbed an enormous bit of a knife and ripped through Newman's uniform and into his arm. Newman struck the fellow flush in the face. Thankfully, he recalled, that blow had sat his combatant on his ass. Both were taken to a military base nearby. The young fellow was the son of a lower-echelon British officer who simply overreacted to Newman's automobile jamming him into a couple of sidewalk merchants.

But aside from the blood and Newman's wounds, a very good show had been put on for all, and the British were without a suspect.

"Thank you, Mr. Newman. I'm sorry about your wound and all of your troubles. The young fellow is quite remorseful about it all, too. But you were quite accomplished in the entire scene. Do you realize that you have all the earmarks of a screen star? What an extraordinary action picture you could make! Someday I would like to make such a picture,

27

but only with your assistance!"

And Mr. Simon laughed and so did Newman, at least until the bandages made him wince. It took four months before Newman left that hospital. He left with his scar, only to return to Boston and to live as an outpatient at the Charlestown YMCA for his wound to more completely heal. But before that he got to have a bit of rest and relaxation in Palestine. And there was a young lady there, too.

The hospital was a rather small, local facility that existed on charitable donations from mostly Christian groups. Newman was on a ward with about a dozen other patients, old men who were recovering from some surgery or another and accident victims much like himself. Agricultural accidents were a part of rural Palestine, and the simplest tractor wrecked havoc on teenage boys, in particular.

But this was when Newman came to know one of the three nurses who attended his ward, a young Scottish woman named Christine McFarland. When Newman's hand ran over his arm and he felt the undulation of his wound, Newman's mind could not help but return to his stay in that tiny hospital outside of the town of Tiberias. But mostly Newman remembered that Scottish girl who had come to the Holy Land on a religious mission. She was no more than five feet three inches tall, and she wore dark-rimmed glasses that made her look like the classical schoolteacher, which she apparently was at one time in her life.

"You really are digging up the past," Newman muttered to no one. Yet it was the mirror in the Charlestown YMCA that directed all of his thoughts.

****

A ringing bell jolted Newman.

"Last stop. Last stop, fella." The operator of the trolley looked perturbed. "This is it. The end of the line."

"Sorry, I must have been in a fog. Are you heading back to

Mystic?"

"In about ten minutes," the conductor remarked looking annoyed.

Does he think I'm drunk, Newman wondered. "I'm going back, so I'll just wait for you. I'm sorry if I've held you up."

The conductor nodded and walked to the back of the streetcar.

Aware of the screeching of trolley-track wheels going along the winding tracks, Newman thought about what his life would have been like had he stayed in Mystic. A job in the Boston area which probably would have been connected to the trolley line - this would have been his life if he had wished it.

As he held onto the rail of the seat in front of him, he noticed that many of the houses he passed were tiny but neat. Flowers decorated the single, double, and triple deckers that were so much a part of the landscape. Other simple but expressive signs of human habitation reached out to him - a potted geranium placed on the top step of a porch, a braided rug sat atop a piazza, a single chair or table situated near the porch railings. All were signs that the folks by the trolley tracks had made their peace with the riders of the trolley. It would be difficult to determine who had compromised the most - the trolley riders or the residents. There remained a view of the saltwater marshes and the tide pools, but one needed to strain to see beyond the highest bushes and over the rolling hills.

As a child, Newman remembered his father taking him for a walk out by the railroad line, and he recalled the fruit trees that dotted the entire railroad line. Everybody had fruit trees. Apple trees had been a must, especially the early fall macintosh. Plum trees were popular. Short, stout pear trees guaranteed a household jams and jellies for the winter. The railroad had replaced the fruit trees. Newman continued to think of the beauty of this place that, in truth, did not exist any longer.

Newman got off the trolley at the top of Ferry Street which left him about a half-mile walk to Suffolk Square. He wanted to walk down a few streets and see some sights before some of the day's obligations were done. Surely, he reflected, he would stop in at Jenny's house and see Mrs. Glass. That would be hard to do, but the time was at hand. An old aunt of his lived just outside the Square, and she too would have to be seen. And he wanted to find out if one of his old pals still lived nearby. But before any of that, Newman wanted to visit the house he had lived in as a boy.

Triple-deckers guarded the entrance to Newman's old neighborhood, as if it were their responsibility to preserve the secrets of the people who had occupied them, or who had lived within them but, long since, moved away. Against the sky, the buildings looked out over the landscape appearing as lonely beacons awaiting inevitable ruin.

Castle Gardens was a complex of apartments that even years ago smelled of trash left out for too long. Painted battleship gray, the three-story tenements were connected, interrupted only by a courtyard. The apartments were tiny but inexpensive. Literally, thousands of families had made their start in America from places like Castle Gardens.

"My father owned these buildings," Newman reflected, "with a local credit union, a little bank that local people subscribed their savings to as a mutual loan society. A distant cousin ran the credit union, a man who had loved Shakespeare more than he had loved debits or credits. The citizens knew that Bernard was the right man to run the credit union, for he was as thrifty with their money as he was with his own. "I don't know if my father made any money with the apartments at Castle Gardens," Newman reflected, "but I do know that my father let people owe him money. Although I was not here, I was told my father died with a million IOU's and a few pennies in cash. I guess the pennies were to be equally divided. I don't remember my father ever talking about dying, not when I knew him. Dying was useless conversation to him anyway, almost as bad as talking about the weather. Only Torah mattered. Only Torah spelled out the purpose and the plan. But I was deaf to my father's message and his pleas." Newman remembered how hard his father had tried to explain that plan to his unwilling fourteen-year-old son, and how difficult it would be to wrestle with the Divine.

Newman approached the top of the street where he had been raised. It was a narrow street in a section that was a mixture of city and suburb which distinguished many older American cities. He remembered the street being busier. In his youth, peddlers had hawked their wares night and day, selling everything including sweet oranges, sweet oranges.

Three-deckers kept the sun from shining on both sides of the street at the same time. As a kid, Newman used to sit on the sunny-side curbstone till about 1:00 pm when the afternoon sun made him switch sides. Walking down the street now, he glanced over at a field where he had once played. Then its grass grew so high that he had imagined it to be what Africa would be like. Into that grass, as a boy, he had dumped a pigeon he had struck dead with the butt of an old BB gun, an unintentional, brainless act.

"Why did you kill that bird?" an indignant neighbor had shouted at him. Not waiting for an answer, the neighbor had instructed him to clean up the mess. In shame, Newman remembered trudging home, having spilled blood, an act that had been a mystery to himself and an abomination of a discovery.

Newman knocked at the front door at 159 Essex Street and gazed upward at the three box-like apartments stacked one atop another. A short, metal fence surrounded the house, something he was sure was not there when his family had lived there. There were bushes out front that had the sparsest number of leaves. Newman tapped three times on the door. A woman answered. She had short, black hair with a front wave that reminded him of a man's haircut. In a most

31

youthful and feminine voice, she asked, "May I help you?"

"Oh, yes. Yes. You see I live here ... used to live here. My family lived here. At least when I was growing up. My name is Jake Newman. Anyway, I was hoping I could just look inside. Just take a look. I've been away for a long time, and - if it's no bother - may I take a look?"

"I remember the name. My husband and I bought this house from the credit union in Suffolk Square, and I think at one time it belonged to a Newman family. Come in. Come in. We've been here about six years, but the place isn't really different than when we first moved in. New paper and paint, and a new stove over there. You take a look."

Newman trailed about the living room and followed the long corridor toward the four bedrooms that had made the place attractive to a family of five girls and a single son.

"My parents, I mean my father and stepmother, had that room. I had that small one down the end. I think I remember that dresser. Has it always belonged to you? Those claw-like feet remind me of the one I had."

"No, that was here. I have a boy who's ten, and he uses it. Was it yours?"

"I think it might have been. That's nice, though. I'm glad it's here. It reminds me of all the time I spent in this room. Is there still a back porch with a high railing? May I go out there?"

And as the two walked out to the porch, Newman recalled the spot where he would sit, sometimes on an old kitchen chair, where he'd read a book and get some glimpse of the world that seemed so far and enchanting.

It was a simple apartment, but it had not been a simple life. "Thanks for letting me in," Newman said and hurriedly waved goodbye. Newman felt queasy as he walked through the Square area of streets, shops, and storefront businesses. He went into the little deli where the man who had served him earlier in the day recognized him and waved. It was an unexpected recognition that Newman appreciated. He

32

smiled then made his way into the bathroom to the side of the restaurant.

The bathroom, a closet-like room, contained a sink and a toilet. Over the sink was a long, rectangular mirror. He recognized the face in the mirror as his own, but it was not an easy recognition. "Like a stranger to myself," Newman thought. He felt as if he been outside of his mind's eye for a decade. Yes, his hair was thinning to the point of extinction, but it was the totality of himself, the totality of his person that defied his memory. He did not recall when his eyes had begun to be so heavy, when crow's feet characterized his face, when his nose had grown so long and lean. This stranger in the mirror made Newman press closer to the glass so that he could see beads of sweat near his sideburns.

A knock at the door startled him. "Anybody home?" a husky voice exploded into the air.

"Be right out." Newman looked again in the mirror, then flushed the toilet.

Waiting outside was a short, dark-haired man in his late forties who looked familiar to Newman. Both men looked hard at one another, as though trying to penetrate the mask that time had inscribed.

"Jakie? Jake Newman?" And Newman stared at the man, stared to unmask a face equally altered by time.

"Sure. Sonny Jurick. My pal, Sonny. How' ya doin', Sonny? I thought that was you. You haven't changed a bit."

"You mean I always looked this old, this terrible?"

They laughed.

"But you, you really do look good. What brings you back here?" Sonny asked.

Before any answer could be given, a half dozen other questions peppered Newman about the past and people that both men had known. For an instant, Newman was glad to see Sonny. He was the son of a local grocer, a friend of Newman's who went back to elementary school. Actually his name was Samuel, but the name hadn't stuck. What Newman recalled was Jurick's smile and the cheery disposition that made him a natural storyteller. His expressive eyes had helped his jokes and his stories. Shorter than he recalled, that smile had not dimmed, nor had the hope which it underscored.

Like a tree that covers its wounds with new growth and thus takes on a changed form, Newman's past appeared before him as though revealed. And yet it seemed as though his life which may have once been a part of him was anything that he recognized as truly a part of him. His past had become alien even to himself.

"Enough of this," he said to no one but himself. "What the hell am I doing here? Someone else should have taken this one. Why me? Coming back here is just kicking up dust that doesn't help anybody."

He didn't feel any better, because he understood his objections were irrelevant. Ok, so he could not help but remember some faces and some people that were part of his past. So what. He was here to remember. He was here to let whomever was interested know that somebody cared and was paying attention. "Big deal," he thought. "Do your job and don't try to relive your life." And that was what Newman tried to tell himself. Do your job. Do your job and then you will get back to New York where you can read the newspapers and pray for Roosevelt to do his job and, who knows, maybe the world will not go into the shit can.

Newman needed hope. You are not alone, he told himself. Eight years of FDR had lifted the spirits of a depression-wracked America, but little in the way of lasting economic improvement or continued hope endured. And Newman knew this, too. At least in New York, Newman thought about Roosevelt. In Mystic, Newman thought about New England, about the ocean, about a little community of people that was actually a speck in comparison to the wider world. But in Mystic, this speck seemed important. And Newman thought it was important, too, although he preferred not to think about that.

All the while Adolph Hitler was fashioning a destiny for the German people and the German nation that called forth anger and terror and a silence of acceptance. The battle-grounds multiplied. People continued to read the newspapers and follow the events of the larger world, but most people did not consider themselves hostages to those news headlines. One country after another, one people after another, fell prey to a wave of German fascism with only England resisting, but that was the larger world.

Here he was in a smaller world, back in the little town just beyond the salt tides. And wasn't it a miniature kind of world, Newman asked himself? Everything looked tiny and built to a scale reserved for a child's train set. Was it New York that made him feel the comparison of size? Was it the way he had spent all those years away from the town?

Maybe it was Newman's realization of how neatly he fit into the town, how conventional he felt his life had become, even in the role of being little more than a visitor. That must be it. How conventional, back in this place, doing a job, even writing his news articles about how a community of people get a hold of their lives.

Newman could no longer put the world on hold, and was that not a sign of how absolutely like everyone else he had become?

Chapter Three

The Message Is Be Strong

When the orders came down from the Director, Jake Newman knew better than to question or delay. The Director's words were law. That was the nature of the Organization of American Hebrew Aid. What needed to be done was as apparent and automatic as the Director's commands. Like a big brother organization or, better yet, a network of big brothers, OAHA monitored the little towns and the cities that fanned out throughout the country. In living rooms, meeting halls, in basements of stores and even churches, the varied lives of American Jews might share a moment, maybe a problem with a man or woman from out of town.

What was there to know? The job was a simple one: to provide comfort and understanding from a large philanthropic organization to needy brethren, be they in Wyoming or aboard a tired, lumbering passenger ship. A band of six case workers, the "Middle Age Sliding and Slipping Rescuers of the World" as they called themselves, five men and a woman, worked their way from ships to trains to bus depots. "The ultimate of the helping professions," Carla was wont to say, creating uproarious laughter among a group who seriously believed in their work.

And it was not only Jews who benefited from the tireless work of the OAHA; immigrants from everywhere - Italians, Russians, Rumanians, Greeks, or whoever searched for understanding - benefited from the organization's work. The OAHA did as much as its tiny staff and a small budget might do to figure out how Jewish communities could master their problems, how families could educate their children or locate a rabbi for a funeral, or simply get enough people together to celebrate the High Holidays in a way that was beyond their everyday lives. Across the United States, in large and small communities in which Jewish life had taken root, festered some of the frustrations and dilemmas of American life, especially for new immigrants who sought reassurance and direction.

America seemed like a great treasure chest for so many of the incoming peoples. The utter variety of things to buy or merely look at intrigued people. Little did the larger American population realize the gratitude these immigrants had for these new beginnings, the kind of gratitude one feels when an injury is attended to by a physician or when some possible calamity finds a relatively easy or harmless solution. This gratitude was matched only by a tenaciousness of spirit, a pent up hunger for recognition and for opportunity so that just a speck of their pent up vitality for life might emerge.

But there was another reality, a reality that echoed America's hunger for the energy and ideas that this tide of new people brought to America. And this was the unhappy fact that prejudice, anger, fear, and mean-spiritedness gripped the hearts of some people who worried about these Jews. In a searing, disruptive frenzy toward human differences was unleashed a bolt of hatred that destroyed the victim and the victimizer, too. That's where Newman came in.

Five days a week for fifty weeks a year and over the last eight years, Jake Newman's life was lived at the entry rooms of passenger ships and train depots. He was the friendly face, the helping hand, the representative of an organization that tried to provide a sense of light for new and not-so-new Americans. His Yiddish got better each year, and he had picked up "hello" and "how can I help you?" in a dozen other languages. A forty-seven year old transplanted New Englander, accustomed to riding out difficult days on perilous seas, Newman examined the world of New York through immigrant lenses.

He was made for this job. Newman said this often. It was a fact, and it was unusual. He was a small-town kid who first ran off to sea. Later, his bones and his muscles were wrought by hard labor, hauling and lugging and learning to survive on boats. And now that all seemed like so long ago.

"I returned to the land," he laughed. It was time to do other things. Even more than that, it didn't matter anymore.

He had been alone long enough to understand that a sign of life is when one crawls on land. That was what needed to be done. To crawl. Belly down, it was time to crawl on land. Crawl and then walk; that mattered and the sea did not matter.

"Just another path but on the same route," Newman liked to think. "Maybe it is even true." He was not afraid of such statements any more than he was afraid of the reality that he was a social worker. Sure, he wrote copy for the little newspaper the OAHA put out, *The Sea of Reeds*, but Newman understood that the paper was little more than a fund-raising arm of the organization.

"You need bait even if you're trying to catch smoke," one of Newman's compatriots was given to say, usually under the influence of a number of drinks.

By-line notwithstanding, Newman was a social worker. His desk and the other desks of his "colleagues in Americanization", another of Carla's phrases, occupied a corner of a floor of the OAHA offices. Two large windows looked out onto the traffic of the city. Only the excess papers and turmoil of Newman's desk adequately mirrored the collective humanity on the streets of New York. Like newspaper reporters, social workers shared information about housing availability, work opportunities, and neighborhoods to make a start for the new families that were part of an endless tide. Ringing in his ears were the words that greeted him, "I have two small children." "My family needs a place to stay." "Have you any word from my cousin, George Kravitsky. He was aboard..."

He felt lucky that his job kept his interest to an extent that even he found curious. He thought of himself as a helper and as a recipient of help. Newman never forgot his own erratic and "quilted" (as he liked to call it) life. "Newman's jobs have been fairly steady. He simply is unsure of any commitment beyond that," Carla was wont to say. And this, too, made Jake and Carla laugh in a kind of sardonic delight. "Sort of like an ancient golem, one of the protectors of the tribes of Israel, but where does the golem go for love-and understanding?"

"Simply to sleep, Carla. One needs to get ready for the next workday, you know."

****

Newman was intrigued by the faces of the people. In the expressions of children, particularly, he recognized a reflection of himself. It was like an early memory that had become lost amid a multitude of more recent memories. His life was like a dream of far- off places and people, exotic and exciting but a life out-of-step with the workings of a family or a place called home. Sure, Newman understood that no destination lived up to its billing.

"Don't get too comfortable," he would tell himself. "Stick to the short term, to the resolutions, the resolutions to the difficulties people experience. That makes sense. Only problem-solving makes sense; that is what he thought. People needed their obstacles demolished or at least ended or seen for what they were. Destinations were a part of some larger mirage. Peace. People needed peace, only peace.

He was deferential toward the people who hung on to his side, relied on his words, and looked at him as though he had filtered the air so that it might be breathed.

Living in a two-room New York apartment, Newman was not a fellow many people envied. Over the past four months, Newman had spent two months "cleaning up the last of the immigrant boats that could make it out of Europe, all but gripped in war with the hating voices of Nazis and Brown Shirts shouting the triumphs of fascism. Two other months had Newman in Rock Springs, Wyoming, working with twelve families who were trying to help try to keep their children connected to a sense of their Jewish identity, something

40

that no one in the community was sure how to do. Newman did not envy himself, always trying to balance the old and the new and the ancient. He did not look upon his job or, for that matter, the world as anything but a problem needing fixing. And he was skeptical about how sturdy, how lasting any of his advice might be.

Long ago he had stopped wondering if he was clever enough and simply honest enough to make any difference in people's lives. He did his job. He had his job. Some good came out of it. That was all that he needed to know.

And there was a drop of something else. Newman understood that he had a front-row seat. "Get a real job," he had been urged by certain acquaintances. "Are you kidding? This is the only real job I've ever had."

He watched thousands move from the health and inspection stations, the terror on their faces equalled only by their joy that the journey was at an end. When necessary, Newman cajoled custom inspectors and public health officials. "Look, pal, this guy is from a little village in southern Italy. I know his cousin. Stamp the card. He's going to work. No public dole for this guy." To ease people into America, that was his job, and that was an end within itself. Self-contained without being self-absorbed, Newman was useful to his clients and even to the customs bureaucrats.

Maybe it was the entry rooms of Ellis Island that most intrigued him. Here he studied the faces of people from a thousand different villages and cities. He looked at babushka-covered heads of girls sixty years away from the faces of their grandmothers, girls and boys intent on the problems they understood their parents had experienced. It was a magnificent panorama, a look at humanity that surpassed a visit to a foreign port. It was as though these people had crossed the Red Sea but were still unsure of the location of the forces of the Pharaoh. "They haven't stopped looking over their shoulders," Newman reflected. "Maybe they believe their past will not free them, and they will have to turn around and have their hopes lifted from their lives, burned like the fog only to reveal an empty horizon."

They were a people in flight and that sense of being pursued continued even after they had arrived. Newman identified with that.

"They run until it is safe to turn around. But when is it safe to do that? And until you turn around, you're never sure whether you can stop running. It is all so confusing," he thought. Desperate people do not receive an ovation for their efforts any more than they receive understanding of their fear. He saw that Americans would rather forget about the immigrants, about so many people lost or left out or merely frozen in time. And the fires that raged within such people seethed, invisible to applause or the naked eye or to intellect, too. And that caused the greatest pain - the assumption that neither intellect nor purpose existed within the frames of such dispossessed souls.

Hate was infectious, Newman believed, but hate was like a seed warmed in the soil of indifference. Here it was fertilized and given the conditions to grow. It did more than spread. Hate took the oxygen out of the air. It robbed the air. It took its toll on the human spirit. "That's it," Newman nodded to no one but himself. "The very act of being human and allowing oneself to be taken up with an idea, a dream, and then hate snares all of that in a sad but predictable way. It has the force of suction, and there lies its power."

It was the blindness of hate that Newman despised. "Unmask it. Unmask it. Rip it away. Unmask it," he thought. Newman understood his role within the organization. In fact he went about his business with a sense of purpose. To him, prejudice was a weapon used against others in a "them versus us" fashion. Newman worked to take that weapon away. Hate was a war to Newman. He was hypnotized by the naked horror that filled people when they were caught in the grip of hate. How many individuals could say that they were a one-man rescue team? How many people had a responsibility for making a kind of deal that affected the lives of countless others? Newman was more than a social worker and a journalist. He thought of himself as the embodiment of the witness, the one that hears the crying out, that hears the calling into the night, the crying for someone to listen. That is what Newman probably did best. He was a simple listener. He listened. When the world had grown deaf or feigned deafness, he was caught up in a stare, in the habit of looking straight ahead.

"I will listen. It is the least I can do. Who can say what can come from listening? It is a beginning."

And by listening, it often seemed that, somehow, Newman evened the score. Whether he actually helped or not, even he did not wish that probed too deeply. But when a person felt that the world had it in for him, because of his accent or the spelling of his name or because Saturday and not Sunday was his day of rest, such a person looked to Newman as a life line. He evened the score. He possessed hope; he offered hope.

****

America was always changing. That was America, a place for change, so much so that America was change itself. Mostly, change came without a hard heart, without resentment or bitterness. There was a silent expectation that change was another opportunity, the next opportunity, a fresh wind that would sweep aside all that had grown stale or unnatural. Change corrected the errors of nature, and America was the place for such corrections to occur.

Change only needed to be put into some kind of formula, some kind of system, so that it could work; that was all change needed and that was what America did best. America unravelled all of the hindrances and obstacles and ill winds of the old world. Change was the opening of the door, and the freshness and naturalness of the land would sweep aside all the imperfections.

Then came the first World War. America was rocked by change; a different, disquieting, and self-absorbing kind of change came with the first World War. The "war to end all wars" may or may not have lived up to Woodrow Wilson's expectations, but the soldiers came home thinking the job had been done. About the only thing that the war stopped was any desire of Americans to give a good damn about what went on overseas. Locking the door and pulling down the shades were uppermost on most people's minds. And there was even more of a dark side or sense of resignation about life than that.

An ugliness had appeared. The twenties in America was a time when speaking one's mind could cost somebody a job, one's health, or whatever else was held dear. Any labor union that wanted any advantage for its members found itself hauled before the courts and across the headlines as either rabble-rousers or Reds. Even the striking Boston Police Department saw its Irish-led police force vilified and then fired. Longshoremen on both American coasts were tainted by Red-baiting or damned as world-threatening anarchists. When the news of the Sacco and Vanzetti trial echoed throughout the nation, more anti-immigrant and anti-labor sentiments filtered their way into people's thinking. Everyday citizens began to suspect that America was a step from being overturned by conspirators and that change itself had been usurped as an alien weapon. Anybody with an accent was a potential enemy of the state; straight- thinking Americans were justified in shutting out foreigners from entering the golden doors of America. The dignity and history of change was in ill repute.

That kind of climate put Jews at a disadvantage. Two million Jews had made their way to the United States from 1900 through about 1925. To many Americans, two million Jews meant trouble. OAHA was founded to combat that misapprehension. And that's how it was that Jake Newman found himself boarding buses and trains, using the New York Public Library as the college library he had never known, learning more about America than this middle-aged man could have imagined.

****

He had an earlier life and that was the way he sometimes referred to it. That was the part of his youth that he spent on merchant marine ships, carrying freight and passengers from one obscure part of the globe to another. That was the time when he preferred the sea to the land, any land, America or anywhere else. In a way, the sea provided Newman the kind of excitement and security that he wanted, living in a way that he wanted his life to go, or what he thought he wanted. He never found himself in any one place longer than it took to load one ship or wait for the second or third ship in port before it was time to pack up, secure the cargo for passage, and head back to sea.

It was hard working aboard a cargo ship. But he enjoyed the work, just as long as there was a bit of peace, too. And that was part of the bargain that the sea always delivered. There was peace or moments of peace. The sea promised and delivered.

"Sort of like the Foreign Legion," the merchant sailors joked among themselves, "a ship is full of odd- balls, all the misfits of America on a pleasure cruise." But to be aboard an ocean-going ship at dawn was a moment that Newman relished. Purple-colored skyscapes, tinged with a fiery red and orange, made Newman halt whatever it was that was before him. He came awake to what was a message of the earth's peace and grandeur. He was a spectator to a kind of opening of the world, and, as often as he experienced such a sight, it continued to awe him. In his mind he reserved that word, awe, for sunrises or sunsets, and he grew unaccustomed to using that word for other sights or sounds or anything in between. In those first few moments when evening turned to daybreak, Newman was transfixed by the sea and sky, and he realized how alive the ocean made him feel.

Newman spent twenty-two years in the merchant marines, and he counted each year as though it were an anniversary or something equally commemorative. "No regrets," Newman stated. "Not many folks get to see the places I've seen - hot lands, cold seas, places that most people stumble over on a map. And that was just the tip of the treat. I've been to those places." Everyplace he had been became a story to be shared with others. They were the living little yarns that decorated his life the way some folks decorate an apartment. Sometimes he jotted down a sentence or two in a schoolboy's notebook and that was all it became, a notebook of passing thoughts; and it was enough to leave it that way. A sailor could keep precious little in gear. Each ship prized its space but not for a seaman's gear. Newman's remembrances became his gear.

But that was long ago. That was before he wanted to be earth-bound, as though he had become a plant within soil. That was why the New York job now fitted into his life. He did what he could with himself, with the life of port towns and port people.

"Who was he, though," he sometimes asked himself. How could he say he lived without an address, without a family, without declaring that he, too, needed to belong to everyday life?

****

An uproar in a small town north of Boston had gained the attention of the Director of the Organization of American Hebrew Aid. It was as though the plight of the community had made its way through prayers more than other means of appeal. There had been short press reports about the incident that the Jewish community was said to have experienced - destruction of Jewish property and physical intimidation, a scourge of the past but in America.

"In many ways, Newman," the Director had explained, "you're the ideal fellow for this one. You're from that town, aren't you?"

Newman was always tense when he spoke to the Director. He was not sure why. Perhaps it was the Director's eyes which, while penetrating, were patient almost to the point of being coaxing. Maybe it was because the Director was so austere in his clothing, his habits, and even in his office furnishings.

"Yes, I was born in that town, but it has been a while since I've been back there."

The Director, a short, stout man, wore a white, long-sleeved shirt unbuttoned at the neck. He wore no tie, nor did Newman recall ever seeing a tie on him. Newman, who sometimes wore a bow tie, thought that the Director most certainly was New York's only chief executive who was without a tie or a suit jacket. In truth, the Director could easily have passed as part of the janitorial staff.

"Whatever. You're the fellow for this; so, please go to that place and see what's up."

The Director was alert; he knew who his staff was, where each was from, and whether the case at hand was right for the person he chose. Just beyond the double picture window in the office, Newman noticed a bowl of water placed on the floor. A long, slender black cat ventured out from under the Director's desk and spotted the Director's lap. He leapt onto it.

"Do you like cats, Newman?"

"Yes, sir. I like all animals."

"Nice. I like that. You like all animals. Nice. This cat sits in the office all day with me. Sometimes she sleeps under the desk on a blanket, or on one of the chairs. In winter, the radiator over there makes a nice corner for her to settle down and soak up the heat."

The cat was jet black except for large, yellow-green eyes and a tuft of white fur under her neck. Newman understood that the Director was fond of cats. "Funny," he thought, "this place is full of regulations on everything from where to hang your coat to when the trash should be put out and how the trash should be bundled, but the Director can keep a cat in his office."

"Newman, this cat keeps me calm. She keeps me aware of all the little things in life that I often take for granted. Sometimes I think she is the link to the real world. You know, the world of nature, lions and lambs, that sort of thing. But has the world got problems. Does it. Always has. All its crazy goings on. I think you have to love the world for what it is. Anyway, that is why I like the cat right here. All I need to do is get her some water, open up a little food for her, and I remember something about myself. It's my pleasure to serve people and cats, too. To serve. Everyone does it, you know. That's totally it. That's the job I see needing to be done. Isn't it odd that a cat can do all that, all the little reminders, almost like a code that explains what's important and what our job is about?"

Newman stepped closer to the Director's desk where the cat had moved. He stretched out his hand and patted the cat on the top of her head. Clearly, the cat had traces of the Siamese breed within it. Her pointy ears, narrow head, and sleek body told that much. The cat enjoyed Newman's touch and kept placing her head by his hands as though this were not the first time they had met and that they were familiar acquaintances.

"She likes you, Newman."

"I love cats. Always have. How old is she?"

The Director chuckled, and the few gray strands of hair at the top of his head bobbed up and down. "Who can say? It seems as though this cat has been with me for quite a while. A dozen years. Yes, I suppose that means she is all of that, a dozen years old. Don't you think she looks well for her age?

How does she look to you?"

"She looks great."

"Newman, every opportunity that involves finding out what makes people tick is filled with uncertainties. I have a feeling that the people in Mystic, who have suffered a disturbance, will be no exception. I suppose there will always be problems with prejudice, even in America; but the beautiful thing about America is here we can actually fix those problems, actually straighten them out. We can show people something about all of us and something about themselves that needs to be fixed. And there's something about all of us that needs fixing. Do you follow me? We all need fixing. We are not into solving people's problems per se, only in dispensing a little understanding. Did you notice that word - dispensing? We do that. Understanding needs to be dispensed; it is medicine. Above all, be strong. You be strong and that will give people direction. So, know what I'm saying?"

"I'll try," said Newman, nodding his head to show that he understood but mostly showing that he heard what was being said.

"That's the way I want you to be."

This serious side of the Director frightened Newman. Newman recognized that the Director knew he was giving him a vast problem, that into his lap was placed a problem bigger than Newman could deal with, never mind resolve.

Sensing Newman's disquiet, the Director softened his tone. "People's feelings are sometimes bizarre, but that remains their endless fascination. Don't you agree? By the way," the director continued, "a young woman died in Mystic. She's a few years younger than you, I recall. Jenny Glass. Did you know her?"

"Jenny Glass?" Newman repeated. Newman looked at the Director, surprised to have heard this name, but hoping to evade some of the emotions he felt.

"How did she die?"

"How? A suicide. She was sick. Clearly it was a suicide,

but how she died does not tell us all that we need to know. We know that she was ill. That is clear. What made her take such a path? That's what I'd like to know. It puzzles me. Ah ... what did I say? Bizarre. Emotions are the puzzles that interest me, sort of as though emotions connect us to one another."

"Yes, I knew her," Newman replied to the Director's question, but he wanted to say nothing else. Newman was diminished by this news. One might believe that Newman was always on the verge of hearing bad news, but this news resounded a depth within Newman that echoed within his mind. And it was more than an echo; it was a hurt, and Newman understood that difference.

Leaving the office, Newman realized that the Director had a confidence in him that Newman himself lacked. To give himself reassurance, he recalled the Director's words. "Prejudice is an insult to the walls of this building."

Still the Director's optimism to the contrary, the record for injustice was real. "Bigotry is a growth industry," Newman thought.

The Director had remarked that as wonderful as America was, and he called it "a unique experiment in the political development of the world", there would always be a place for the kind of services that OAHA could provide. "Do you see, Newman? Do you sense what your role happens to be? Some may call you a troubleshooter. To me you are the reminder, and most of the time that is all that is required - a little reminder."

Newman left the meeting with a somewhat different interpretation. "The Director wants me to do more than provide some public relations service. This was a set up." Mystic was the town of Newman's birth, a place better forgotten than anything else. Now he was about to go back and dig up all kinds of things.

"Perfect for the job," Newman said aloud. "He wants a middle-aged guy to dust off a life that is better left covered with dust."

Newman shook his head. "This is perfect," he repeated. "An old town with old problems. It just happens to be the place I came from."

Newman again recalled his meeting with the Director. "In many ways, Newman," the Director had explained, "you're the ideal fellow for this one. You're from that town, aren't you?" And then, "Jenny Glass. A suicide. Did you know her? Did you know her?"

****

Fortunately, the train trip to Boston did not get rolling until Newman had nestled into a small but empty two-passenger compartment. Trains were a passion for Newman. He thought what a pleasure it was to sit and look out while the countryside rolled by. His B&M compartment had dark, red leather upholstery. The drawn window shades made the temperature in the compartment comfortable.

"On the way to Boston, huh pal?" said a rotund man with a sharp widow's peak of brown hair as he was dragging two large suitcases into the compartment. Newman's sense of solitude on the train had ended. Moving laterally, the broad-backed passenger hoisted one bag over what would be his seat and with a "do you mind?" heaved the other over Newman's seat. Newman's bag was squeezed into a corner of what had now become a cramped space. Smiling, the new-comer seized Newman's small hand with his enormous one.

"Yes, I'm going to Boston," Newman finally got out of his mouth. "You, too?"

"Yeah, I got a cousin who lives up in Hyde Park. This guy gets himself elected a rep or some other phoney-baloney job on Beacon Hill every other year. So I go and visit him, and then we head down to the Cape for a couple of days. His wife and their kids, five of them, have already been there for a couple of weeks. Dennisport ... great place, warm water, great

51

even with the kids! I make this trip every year. We were great pals as kids growing up."

Newman had received a more detailed response than he had bargained for, but he listened politely and with a greater interest than he was willing to admit. All the while, Newman nodded and could not help but be aware of the man's large teeth, somewhat yellowed as though cigars were the great passion of his life.

"Great," Newman blurted out, cutting the guy off from whatever else he was going to volunteer. "Great down the Cape. Say, I'm sorry, but I'm really tired. I think I'll nod off for a bit."

"Sure. Sure, pal. I'm going to grab some z's myself. Know exactly what you mean. If the snoring gets to you, just give me a whack. I've got to sackout."

Gratefully, Newman leaned back into the corner of his seat.

"Eh pal? The name's Lewis, Donny Lewis."

"Jake Newman."

They nodded and drifted back to their separate thoughts. The train did its work cutting into the countryside. Green and lush were the western Massachusetts towns and farmland. As a child Jake had never realized the rural nature of his state. Growing up, he had thought all Masssachusetts cities and towns were like Boston; he had never seen the long, string- like roads that meandered through small town after small town. And between the roads were farms and forests that made him realize how country-like so much of New England actually was.

"Was I nine or ten?" Newman asked himself, trying to realign his age to an image of his physical size."It had to be something like that," he reasoned. He remembered the slogan, "Boston's Best Donuts", and the place that had been run by the Bertoni brothers, Babe and Gene. Though five years younger, Gene weighed about 270 pounds while Babe was a slimmer 250. "There's a lot of meat on the hoof between those guys," he remembered the customers saying while at the coffee counter, while Newman eyed the racks of freshly baked donuts.

Newman could visualize the brothers in white tee shirts and aprons, the only clothing Newman had ever seen them wear even on the coldest days of winter. They looked like twins decked out in their bakers' white, and this perception was reinforced by the outbursts of laughter and disgust which occurred in tandem. Heads tilted to one side, they wiped the counters of crumbs and coffee splatters with the same swish of their hands. The donut stop was their mutual kingdom on the road to Boston.

An enormous truck tire was strapped to the top of the flat roof of the donut shop, just above the doorway. To re-enforce its meaning, a sign above the doorway read "Boston's Best Donuts".

"What was it that we did?" Newman asked himself. "Oh, I remember now. Jim and I got up on the roof one summer's evening and proceeded to climb to the top of that tire. Shimmying up the tire was like climbing a boulder. It was worth it though. At the top of the tire, we could see Beacon Hill and the State House dome sparkling gold in the twilight. I remember being above the tree tops and waving to the ant-like people who spotted us."

The scene became so vivid to Newman that he could hear the words that had been spoken.

"You! Get down from there! Get down! Get down!" Babe's voice had risen in indignation. "I'm going to murder you boys. Do you hear me? Get down from there. I'm going to murder the two of you!" Knowing that Babe was one to live up to a threat, the two of us carefully worked our way down, only to receive a kick in the ass from Jim's father, a burly fellow, who set pipelines for the gas company. Mr. Spinney assured Babe that his son and his friend would pay the price for their foolery. "You boys crazy? Jim, you crazy or something?" he had asked.

"A mere 'get out of here' from Mr. Spinney saved us from Babe's rage," Newman reflected. Nothing remained from our adventure but Mr. Spinney's scrutiny of our actions from that day forward. "Those boys are a bit whacky, if you ask me," Jim had heard him say to one of his co-workers on the gas company crew.

Chapter Four

Beckah Collier

Newman carried a large, blue cloth suitcase into the Converse Hotel. Outside the hotel was the streetcar line which led to Boston. Its encroaching tracks occupied the middle of the street into the heart of Suffolk Square.

Although the Square had grown in size and in the number of people and shops who lived or carried on business there, it possessed the ambiance of the Suffolk Square that Newman remembered. There were the weather- beaten clapboard buildings, mostly one level in height, with prominent large-windowed storefronts that allowed for a quick visual inspection of whatever was inside. Signs were everywhere - words and pictures attempted to exalt one tiny enterprise from a competitor two or three streets removed.

A small man of fifty by the name of Ginsburg owned and operated the hotel. With slick hair combed from front to back and glasses that rested on his nose, Ginsburg possessed a scholarly air. Upon seeing him, Newman was taken by his air of competence, his shirt pocket bulging pencils and at least two pens, all underneath three or four cigars. Ginsburg was a most congenial fellow, his conversation punctuated by an easiness of language that made Newman feel quite comfortable in talking to him.

Mr. Ginsburg's English was laced with the Yiddish expressions of the Jewish immigrants. "As long as one has one's health, Mr. Newman, that is most important," Ginsburg professed, making a motion with his hands as though he were cleaning crumbs from a table. The effortlessness of the movement echoed the commonly accepted words and the wisdom of those words. "Don't you agree?"

"Of course," Newman replied in Yiddish, echoing the sincerity of his host. "All else is temporary. As long as there is our health, what more can we ask of God? The rest is up to us."

"You know of our funeral? Are you a member of the family?" Ginsburg asked and then revealed the specific time and place of Jenny's funeral.

57

"No, not a member of the family, but I knew her once, and I am interested. After all, aren't we members of the human family? You know, members from the same tribe?"

Ginsburg liked what Newman was saying and clearly he possessed similar notions. "What, whatever, Mr. Newman, whatever. Of course. Maybe not one large happy family but certainly part of the great tribe."

"Every funeral is sad, but this one is especially sad. The sickness of the mind is at least as tragic as the sickness of the heart. All sickness remains a sickness. You know, there was talk of burying Miss Glass on the fringes of the cemetery. That would be the custom, you know. But thankfully, such an idea did not prevail. She will be laid to rest in a family plot, not on the border but in the heart of the cemetery, thanks be to reason. Troubles, troubles, troubles! It will take place today. If you like, you can watch the procession to the cemetery right from your room. Over there, across the street is the Harvard Street Synagogue. The procession will circle the Square and stop by its doorfront. Thank you for staying with us. I must go, but it is a pleasure to have you with us." He hurried off through a door behind the front desk, leaving the lobby vacant.

Newman carried his bag up the three flights of wooden stairs. Braided rugs dressed up the stairs and landings. Gold lamps were placed strategically along the hallway. Once in his room, Newman took off his light-blue, summer jacket. Face down, he lay on the double bed and closed his eyes. He felt his legs loosen. The day's journey was over. Although he did not want to fall asleep, he allowed himself to doze and daydream.

****

Effortlessly, he recalled the hot summer days of his childhood. He would walk between the rows of corn stalks that he himself had planted in his backyard. Even though a city kid,

Newman had been fascinated with growing plants, an activity his immigrant parents and larger family looked on as his hobby. To young Newman, the growing of vegetables was more than a hobby. He lost himself in walking between his plants, revelling in the escape and the privacy that his garden offered him. Those were quiet afternoons. When the wind gave a slight sway to the corn, he could feel the warm air of August pass over his face. That heat provided Newman a sense of peace and security as a child, so much so that even as an adult Newman gained strength from the memory.

His father was a contemplative, sensitive man, and a man who spent his life in study or prayer or in commitment to the problems of the countless people like himself. His stepmother, stocky and on the short side, seized every opportunity to turn work into money for the family. In Newman's memory, his parents were always getting ready to go off to their respective jobs while warning him and his sisters to exercise care. "Lock the door. Be careful. Here is some money for an ice cream. The key will be hidden here. Be careful. We'll be home a bit later."

Only the garden had been a place that Newman felt was uniquely his. Only the garden had been free of the worldly entanglements and expectations that a family life wove.

In his dozing, Newman sensed that a window across the room was open. Street noise interrupted him a moment, but it was not enough to rouse him. His thoughts returned to remembrances of his stepmother's voice. In Yiddish, she would seek to clarify some of the ways of the Gentile world versus the ways of Jewish life, so much of this embodied in the ambiguities of American-Jewish life. "You must know that as a Jew you cannot do what others do. Our food is different, just as our everyday lives remain different."

Was it the smells in the kitchen that first suggested to me that she might be right? Did I prefer to believe that there was a touch of an ancient prejudice on her part that needed

59

to be exposed? Or was there something real about the aromas of a kitchen that forces a stranger to understand the heart and the head of those in the kitchen?

"Our strength, may it please God to grant us, is for the life of our children. For you so that your lives will be worth something. To us that means that you stand up for what you are, that you do not forget who you are. That is part of living, a great task in living. That is why we work and toil."

And it was toil, young Newman recognized, that had set his folks and himself apart. "But don't all people toil?" he asked, believing that toil must be constructed within an individual's life.

"The toil of a Jew is held in disdain by the larger world," Newman would one day write. It was not a new idea, just a slant on his upbringing that he had never left behind.

When Jake worked with families, immigrant families, families who lived in cities or in the country, families that were whole or families that were broken, Jake would think of his family, of his people. "We open the earth. America will recognize us. America will recognize the toil of families like mine." Jake's childhood had been like the prairie he loved to read about - open and expansive, full of dreams and aspirations, endless in sky and in mystique. Each family plants and toils, weeps and toils. Each family toils.

A chatter of voices came through the open window. Newman rose from the bed, noticing in the mirror that the bedspread design had made its impression of a small row of flowers across his forehead. He wrinkled his face and moved his jaw hoping to gain control over his face. Outside the window, a funeral procession was passing. In an old, black limousine the family members led the procession. Behind that was a horse-drawn cart carrying a pine box. A hundred people trailed behind. It took only seconds of watching for Newman to realize that this was Jenny's funeral. It was making its way through the town, stopping at the front door of each of the synagogues within the town, before it proceed-

60

ed to the cemetery.

Jake looked out his hotel window, and a breeze touched his face, refreshing him in a way that his brief nap had not. But the heat was there. Almost no one walked the sidewalks of the Square though all the shops were open. Occasionally someone would leave a store carrying a bundle or holding on to a shopping bag containing food.

****

He awoke needing to wash up. His roomy bathroom consisted of a toilet and a sink, broad enough to contain on its rim all of the shaving gear Newman possessed. A claw-foot tub hugged a wall. Newman was satisfied, for he loved the water. He loved to swim as much as he enjoyed a bath. "This will do nicely," he thought and placed a shaving brush and a sharp razor on a small shelf under the medicine cabinet. After running the water, he slid easily into it. Soon steam enveloped the room, relaxing him and making his mind wander some distance from the present.

He imagined himself in a larger tub filled with fragrant spices. "That would be a luxury," he thought to himself, his body and his mind drifting. The feel of the water brought an ease to him. Then his mind reminded him where he was, and he could not help but think how his youth had prepared him for who he was and the tasks he had to do.

He remembered walking through a park one summer where a game of baseball was in progress. Suddenly, a heavy boy had punched and fallen on top of a skinny kid Newman knew as Morton. Dougie, the boy on top, was known as a rough kid; none of the kids, or at least the more savvy ones, ever confronted him. This park crowd thrived on confrontation. It took only a few seconds of watching the fight for Newman to understand that Morton was on the verge of thoroughly having the shit kicked out of him, and maybe more than that.

"Get off of there!" his voice commanded.

Looking up at him, scarlet in the face from combat, Dougie screamed, "Screw you, Jew boy. Is this Jew boy here a friend of yours?" Dougie's neck-lock on his victim intensified, as if any challenge to what was taking place was grounds for intensifying Dougie's ardor and the punishment he meted out.

Newman repeated, "Just let him go. You've got nothing to prove." And then came those words which Newman identified as challenging. "Everybody already knows you're an ass! Just some big gorilla, maybe without a brain."

Flying off his prey, Dougie seized Newman by his shirt collar, squeezing the buttons of his shirt until they were part of a single knot. "You, Jew boy, are going to get your ass kicked."

Newman's left hand knocked Dougie on the side of his whiffled head, then returned to hit his nose. The hit unravelled his crumpled collar, but the shirt did not come back to life. Blood spurted down the redhead's tee shirt. Furious, Dougie hit Newman with a strong punch that landed on Newman's shoulder. Out of nowhere, another punch hit Newman on the side of his face. Newman smashed a blow to Dougie, head high, striking his nose that forced him backwards; then a slight shove landed the redhead on the ground.

"You are an ass," Newman repeated. He had to endure only one more "screw you" while he and Morton made their exit from the park. Newman smiled as he remembered that, in fact, the thankless Morton was a complete fool also. No thanks, no goodbye, nothing that signified a recognition that someone had reached out to help him, and Morton went on his way.

Newman's soap was lost somewhere in the tub, and his reverie was over. Business called. A last gaze at the water draining from the tub was all the leisure that could be permitted.

He dressed, finally slipping on a lightweight sport coat

and proceeded to lock his door.

"You are the representative of the Jewish agency," a voice greeted Newman after he had gone a few steps. "I'm Beckah Collier. My husband is Michael Collier. He's a local business-man who's quite involved in the town and the Jewish community. I take it you came here for the funeral."

She was a tall woman but youthful to the extent that she seemed very much a girl. Maybe she was in her late thirties, Newman thought. She had reddish-brown hair that was pushed away from her forehead. Her dress, shoes, and handbag suggested that she was well-to-do. Actually, she reminded Newman of New York - professional looking and business-like. And there was something directly to the point about her conversation.

Newman was puzzled by her name. "Collier?" he thought. "That's a strange name for a Jew. And her husband is active in Jewish affairs?"

To her question, Newman replied, "Yes, I was at the cemetery. Was the entire service at the grave side?"

"That was the way that Jenny wanted it. All at the grave site. It was the way that Jenny's mother, Mrs. Glass, remembered her talking about it. That might have been just talk, you know, the kind of talk that everybody sort of mentions at one time." Mrs. Collier's eyes displayed more than an interest in conversation or even exchanging information. There was a forlorn look in her eyes, a certain sadness, genuine and quite expressive when she talked. Newman sensed this earnestness in her voice. It was the kind of sincerity that could not be masked nor played at because it was mirrored within the gleam of her eye.

"Were you a friend or a relative of Jenny's?" Newman questioned.

"Yes, I was a friend. It took some time, but we became friends, quite good friends. We worked together as Sunday school teachers at one of the synagogues in town. We had met before that, but that's really where we got to know one another - teaching Sunday school. Sometimes we spent hours just talking about the kids, our lives, the kind of things people talk about I guess. I also worked with her and some of the Boston groups that were trying to get some help to organizations involved in international relief and resettling refugees, especially helping the Jews in Europe where the Germans and the Fascists had left their mark. Jenny was active in those kind of things."

"I remember your name now. Jenny had mentioned you a number of times. You were her childhood friend, the kindred spirit, maybe even more ... at least to her," Beckah added.

"You seem to know more than I do. But that is what makes a small town a small town, I guess. You're right, though, Jenny was a special friend growing up around here. I'm glad she remembered me."

"She did. She remembered you and always in a nice way. You were one of the pleasant memories. I don't mean to make it more or something different from what it was. Forgive me; we'll have to talk about it sometime."

But the young lady had more on her mind. Newman sensed a kind of shifting of gears which was visible on her face. "First, I must tell you that my husband says that you're in town for the wrong reasons and especially at the wrong time. Why stir up the community exactly at a time when the community needs to be reserved and even restrained, especially the Jewish community? He says that with the depression, a war going on, and fear of the United States getting into it, it's sort of a bad time to get people excited. Are you a troubleshooter of some kind, Mr. Newman, or is that troublemaker?"

There was something about Beckah which interested Newman. Yes, she was attractive, but it was more than that. There was a directness to what she said, not an insulting directness, but one that probed as though she sought more than simple answers. Her questions revealed a degree of earnestness, a clear outstretched appeal for some truth to which her pointed remarks were but an appeal.

"You know, it's too hot to look for trouble, and New England is too beautiful to even think of trouble. You've got the ocean and that golden dome on Beacon Hill and all this pretty countryside. Trouble is the last thing I've got on my mind. Lemonade, that's what's on my mind. I'm not here for the scenery and the hospitality. And I'd like to know how a group of old folks got themselves whacked by some other group of people. I grew up in this little town and around Suffolk Square, and I'm curious about things. Does that sound like a troublemaker to you? Curious guy that I am, I just wonder where your husband got that idea." Newman's tone was almost brusque, as though he didn't care, but he did care at least a bit.

Newman didn't want to take this line of inquiry further; however, Mrs. Collier was not quite satisfied.

"This town has many sons and daughters of Mystic's first Jewish families ... families that have done rather well financially. Some have the makings of doing even better when the depression is a memory. Someday the depression will go away; maybe Hitler will go away, too."

"...just like that," Newman interjected. "You really think that problems are like weather patterns. You just wait for the wind to change, and the problems will float on by?"

"Maybe someone will figure out a way to get rid of all the problems ... get rid of Fascism without getting into a war." Mrs. Collier looked less than confident in this exchange, but she continued her analysis.

"Depressions hurt some folks and help others. Real estate, land, everything from chocolate bars to soap detergent ... somebody around here is involved in it and looking to go about with their lives and their dreams. That includes my husband."

"And you? Are you eager to go on, as you say, with your life and dreams, Mrs. Collier?"

"Of course, Mr. Newman. And I'm sure that you are, too.

A life and dreams ... we all want that." Mrs. Collier was articulate, and she was far from defensive.

The more Newman listened, the greater his sense that Mrs. Collier possessed a remarkable poise and even an ability to think of herself beyond the everyday concerns that she expressed.

"Mr. Newman, one of the realities about this town is that it's loaded with S.O.B's. - sons of the boss. Does that have a certain flavor, a certain sense of who matters and what matters around here? I think it does. How politics affects Michael, my husband, or someone similar to him, that is what matters. Some people around here call it the Galileo Complex; the son of the boss is the center of the universe and everything else is child's play."

She and Newman laughed, but Newman enjoyed the kind of detachment that Mrs. Collier showed. He found it interesting not only because it was full of irreverence, but because he believed her words to be searching and exploring and even reaching out. She had courage.

What was Mrs. Collier's point? Newman tried to summarize. The hard work of successful first generation people, all kinds of people, gave way to the preservation instincts of the next generation. Sometimes, but far from always, the sons and daughters found it expedient to lay low on matters of learning or community pursuits or, sadly, basic connectedness. Newman reasoned that this "sons of the boss" autocracy, as he cynically observed, lost interest and even respect for the mind and the soul, too.

"The greatest goal was to be successful, heedless of the spirit of life. Five thousand years after its origins, one long trip through the desert having been recorded, another challenge to the roots of identity cloaked itself in the guise of brokering for success." As this imagery filtered through his mind, Newman recognized the he was bordering on the edge of making judgments about other people that he wished to restrain. Only his own inherent weakness as a person pre-

66

vented him from stopping.

And Newman took his point of view a step further. "And what was the dream? As long as the proprietor of an establishment increased his gain one hundred fold over that of any other laboring person, the world operated properly? Was this what Jenny found herself snickering at ... a certain fantasy, a grabbing and pushing for the golden ring, as though success had replaced all other purposes for living. Success, was that the ultimate commandment?"

Only Mrs. Collier's smile interrupted Newman's own pointed reverie. "I'm sure we'll see one another again" and with these words she drifted into the sidewalk of traffic. But Newman was left thinking about her. In a few moments, however, Newman's mind was elsewhere. As his eyes trailed her heading down the Square's streets, he also caught sight of an endless number of signs, their Hebrew letters identifying grocery stores and butcher shops.

He recalled that the ghetto nature of life in this town was similar to that of many American cities that welcomed the outpouring of emigrant peoples. The Italians and the Slavic people, the Greeks, and the East European Jews who had fled the pogroms and intolerances of countries in which they had lived for three and four hundred years, they all came to America seeking refuge. This made him pause.

"All that those people wanted out of America was a chance to escape the endless limitations and restrictions of Europe. They wanted an end to the dreaded violence and to see their children grow into adulthood." These were Newman's observations.

And he was conscious of all the scapegoating going on in the United States, the despair of the Depression, and the rantings of Father Charles Coughlin and the other haters who were striving to make America a society in which hate and prejudice were accepted and esteemed as a kind of wisdom. That's what the haters wanted for America; it was what gave racism credibility, and it was a disease.

The streets of most major cities in America had placard-carrying despots who brandished a hateful message. Like a tapestry, Newman believed that his efforts were linked to all the madness that was increasingly acceptable. And it was in that competition against that wretchedness that Newman struggled.

He was conscious of his job. "If it takes organizing people, even Jews grown unaccustomed to organization or collective action of any description, then that is what I will do."

Newman tried to focus on the words of the Director. "Your task is to make sure these folks can go about their business. Simply that. I will take care of the obstacles, just carry the message."

Newman's job was to do the Director's bidding as though that rotund little man were a prophet from another age. "That's what the Director thinks he's got," thought Newman, "some kind of messenger."

Newman knew his job about as well as anybody might. Whatever the problems he would face in Mystic, they could be no worse than they had been in other places he had been. Wherever people had been out of work for long periods of time, places such as Detroit and Chicago, those were the places where anti-Semitism or race riots or some intolerance rose up as a sign. Ethnic neighborhoods throughout the nation were hostage to the despair that ran through American life from the factories right across the Great Plains.

Hitler's admirers were spread across the nation, waiting for a signal that validated all their hatreds. Maybe it would be a Franklin Roosevelt appointee whose ancestry triggered an ethnic insecurity. Perhaps Eleanor Roosevelt would make an appearance at a racially mixed gathering or even on behalf of a racial minority. It did not take a whole lot of insti-gation to make America's bigots burn crosses, beat up Jews, terrorize sharecroppers, intimidate academics, and hoist a Nazi banner as a symbol of their rage.

It seemed that every day pictures of the haters, or their words, screamed from the mastheads of newspapers. Who were they? From American Nazi's to reincarnations of some religiously inspired inquisition, the venomous haters emerged: William Dudley Pelley's Silver Shirts; Reverend Gerard B. Winnrod and his Defenders of the Christian Faith; Gerald L. K. Smith; Joe McWilliams; Lawrence Dennis; Father Edward Lagle Curran ... the list grew ever lengthy.

Horrifying reports from Europe challenged a nation replete with domestic bigots at least equal to what was on the European continent. At least that was what Newman suspected.

Newman grew tired for a moment, wishing that a longer nap or a peaceful bath could again interrupt the afternoon, but it was not meant to be. The sun was high, and the heat was as heavy and enveloping as it gets in New England. He had a certain expectation about being back in Massachusetts, for he was always proud of Boston and the state. There actually was a changeless quality about the cities and towns that surrounded Beacon Hill. Newman enjoyed thinking about how so many surrounding hills provided just the right height to peer upon the Charles River Basin and the golden dome of the Boston State House. Boston was a place full of academic stature and a financial center for much of New England. Boston was the Hub. Newman was nurtured on that proposition.

Here, at a hotel he vaguely recalled, he prepared himself for all the difficulties he was about to face. His role would be to make it difficult to steamroll irresponsibility through this community. The morning newspaper was his wake up call, but his duty was here.

As he thought about the marshes and flatlands that led to the sea from the hotel that he now called home, he recalled the paths that he walked as a boy down to the ocean. He followed the railroad lines that cut through a couple of other towns that passed by the seashore, and he remembered visiting the ocean birds and the clammers and the old lobster-men, bundled up against the cold ocean even on summer mornings.

"Hey lad ... yes, you lad. Don't go thinking the ocean's your friend. It is not; rest assured of that. You keep your feet on the land, and don't go thinking how you'd love to be at sea. The sea is trouble. Do you hear? Trouble. The sea does not make you free. That is a myth and one of the greatest lies of all time. The sea is a no man's land; it's not some place to play or even a place where a man can earn a living. It's a loser's life. Did you hear? It's a loser's life out here, not for anybody who belongs anywhere or belongs to anybody. Stay put. Do you hear? Stay put where you are right now!"

That was what those old guys would yell out to me. Wasn't it? With some strain, Newman sought to remember.

Chapter Five

Make A Miracle

The Capitol Theatre, a two-story building just outside of Suffolk Square, was the place where the Jewish community gathered to watch a travelling vaudeville show or an occasional Yiddish performance. Mostly, it was used as a movie theatre. Especially on the weekends, the Capitol was packed. Even when movies were being shown, the outside sidewalk and steps leading into the building were flowing with human traffic. Like all of Suffolk Square, the cobblestone streets carried an ongoing chorus of voices, footsteps, and the rolling iron of delivery carts.

But there was quiet in the Square this evening. This evening, by six o'clock, it was packed with subdued and quiet children, young adults who seemed more than a bit serious in bearing, and older folks who spoke in hushed tones.

Three chairs had been placed on the stage. There was a dark velvet curtain behind the chairs, but there was nothing else. Despite the orderliness and an uncommon solemnness, this was a disheartened gathering. Perhaps there was an undercurrent of anger, but it was an anger of disillusionment. Newman looked at their faces, and he listened to the meandering silence, and he understood the people's pain.

As he sat near the back of the theatre, just in front of an ornate set of seats in a corner niche, Newman listened to the chatter. There was talk of those persons who had been injured and of other persons who were terror struck. There was talk of fear and of anger. Individual witnesses stood to give testimony.

"May I tell you what I saw?" said a well-dressed woman. She stood and with a dispassionate voice she spoke, "I saw three of them grab Mr. Greenfield and kick him to the ground. Broken glass was outside his store. So were the windows of the fish market, the butcher shop, a pharmacy, and Mr. Berman's dress shop - all smashed. They just went from shop to shop, pushing people out of the way, calling out names like 'kike' and 'bagel', and yelling, 'Get out of our town!' 'We are taking what belongs to us,' one of them shouted as he reached into the window of the pharmacy, taking a window display! Can you imagine?"

"I saw the police, two policemen, just watch them. Even when they struck a person, even then, the police did nothing. This was not something they were going to get involved with. We shouted for police, but they did not move. Can you believe this? They did not even try to control them? The police were worse than anybody. Like Cossacks! They allowed them to break the windows and then the police tried to break our heads."

Newman noticed that even though two months had passed since the incident, people still carried signs of the riot with them. One individual, who sat with the older citizens in the front of the auditorium, had bandages wrapped around his forehead; another, who sat two seats in back of him, had his arm in a sling. But it was the anger that had not abated. These people believed that they had been victims of terror. Newman was struck by the rage that the incident had provoked.

"This is not Russia!" Newman heard someone say. Another voice rose above the rest. "We will fight them! They'll see; we'll fight them. We won't take it!"

A tall, young man rose from the audience and went up the steps to the middle of the stage. "I'd like to call this meeting to order," he began. "Please. Could we come to order. Tonight we have a report from our representative to the court proceedings, Mr. Jacobsen, and we also have another speaker. Please come to order and let the business proceed."

The audience settled into silence as the representative, a man about sixty years-old, made his way from the audience to one of the chairs on stage. He was totally bald and casually dressed in a white, short- sleeved shirt. Newman noted that he spoke with a lisp, and his hands were quite expressive. Clearly, he had the attention of the assembled.

Solemnly, he reviewed what had happened up to now. "On a summer, Sunday evening at about eight-thirty, the Jewish neighborhood, which is surrounded by a square of shops and tenements, was quiet. It had been," he went on, "a day of people walking about, talking on streetcorners, strolling with children - a typical Sunday before the normal work week. Into this peaceful scene, some forty males, aged sixteen to thirty, marched down the two central streets of the Square in a phalanx. They broke the windows of shops and assaulted individuals as they moved to the center of the Square. At the time, there were no police in the Square or on patrol. A call for police went out on the nearby police box, but police response was slow; and for approximately forty minutes, time seemed suspended. People wondered, 'Was this attack a pogrom?' All the words of the pogrom filtered through the summer's evening. 'The Jews must go! Kill Kikes.'"

"We're going to show them!" a woman's voice rang out from the audience, interrupting the speaker. The voice belonged to an older woman wearing black eyeglasses. She stood. "No one is going to tell us what we can do! We'll show everyone that we cannot be intimidated." There was applause for the woman who helped rouse a certain passion within the most timid spectators.

Other members of the audience now commented on the police who had acted as if in slow motion with a wry smile on their faces, performing their jobs with indifference to broken glass and horror-stricken faces.

Mr. Jacobsen then went on with his report saying, "Four arrests had been made; later, sixteen others had been arrested. All the arrested were referred to in the local newspaper as the 'marsh lads', coming from the Irish enclave of Edgeworth."

Newman knew of Edgeworth. It was a section that was as poor as Suffolk Square, twice as old, and filled with second and third generation Irish who labored in the tanneries, paint factories, and rubber boot companies. Some streets of Edgeworth were paved; others were not. When it rained, much of Edgeworth became a rutted series of soggy roadways. In Edgeworth, it was understood that Irish laborers would give a lifetime of labor for the barest of wages. Without being told, Newman imagined what had happened. Poor Irish had assaulted poor Jews.

The representative continued to summarize the events that followed the riot. After a week of testimony in a packed courtroom, fines of $50 and suspended sentences had been levied against the four arrested youths.

The audience followed the recitation of the events with total involvement. They responded with questions, rhetorical and philosophical, challenging anything positive about their assailants or the police. Bitterness so affected the crowd that the chairman, Mr. Joruchoff, asked for cooperation and silence so that the report could be concluded.

Mr. Jacobsen described the defense of the assailants. "As many of you know, the defendants' attorney argued before Judge Prebble at the District Court that they were set upon by old men with whiskers who proceeded to beat them and forced them to defend themselves. The defendants maintained that they were harmlessly passing through the Square when attacked. Lt. Colley of the police department characterized the youths as 'marsh lads', well known to the community and no more anti-Jewish than the larger community."

There were gasps from the listeners. The representative went on. "Attorney Laban Morrison of the Suffolk Square neighborhood, in his argument for the prosecution, said, 'This attack is part of a long- standing tradition of harassing and terrorizing the local Jewish community. The intent of this abuse,' he went on, 'is that the Jews will leave the area and extinguish whatever Jewish institutions exist. Children are carrying out the work that their elders have only whispered about. It is kitchen-table hatred. Kitchen- table talk has brought on a night of horror!'"

Jacobsen returned to his chair on the stage. Still acting as moderator, Joruchoff introduced the second speaker. "We have with us a representative from the Organization of American Hebrew Aid from New York. He would like a few moments to discuss this situation with us. I know you will welcome him. Please, Mr. Newman, Mr. Jake Newman, will you come up to the stage?"

As Jake walked from the rear of the hall, his stomach began to churn. Newman was not frightened by such encounters, but writing about a public gathering was different from talking to people looking for direction. "This part of the job doesn't suit me," he had mentioned more than once to the Director.

The Director had put the duty this way. "Think about talking to crowds as if you're just repeating what needs to be said. Figure out how they can make peace with themselves. Help them get the message. What other help can we offer? It is the only real help they need, a confidence that all will be well."

Jake stood on the stage in front of the crowd. Only then did he realize how hot it was. A large fan hung from the ceiling, but it helped only the people in the front of the mezzanine. Smaller, standing fans had been placed around the theatre, but they were mostly ineffective. Jake's sport jacket took on a darker blue hue as sweat poured from him, drenching his shirt. However, the heat was the least of his difficulties. Though his body was uncomfortable, he sought to make his mind relaxed and open to the problems that the evening would bring.

"Ladies and gentlemen, my name is Jake Newman, and I'm from the Organization of American Hebrew Aid. It's my pleasure to be with you to let you know that you are not alone and that the issues that concern you concern many, many people. First, I'd like you to know that my organization is set up to help bring to light some of the problems which beset communities throughout the United States. What are these problems? Those difficulties that stem from prejudice and poison that make some folks feel that they have rights that are more important than other people's rights. That attitude cannot exist in a democracy. No one is going to stand for violence showered on a people because of their religion or race. That's out of bounds, and our organization is well equipped to take such violations to court, before the American public, and to the halls of Congress itself."

Jake could feel that the crowd was listening. A few applauded his words.

"But we do not make miracles. Miracles are not called for to solve most problems, especially problems in America. Maybe because so many people, including the leadership of my organization, believe that America itself is a miracle. We are interested in making the miracle of America work - work for you and for all people."

A respectful silence followed his words, but Newman heard some grumbling, too. Did they think he was wet behind the ears? Was he more of a "greenhorn" than many in the audience, he wondered.

He continued, "I'm not here to give you all the answers or make promises that I cannot keep. My job is to bring your problems out into the open, under the light of question and scrutiny. For it is the truth which is the only weapon we possess. We should not be afraid of the truth, regardless of where it leads or whom it confronts. We cannot wander from the truth any more than we can wander away from our enemies. That's not part of our agenda. My job over the next couple of weeks is to help the community make peace with itself and to do what is possible. This means that we will continue to seek redress in the courts and through the law. The law means a great deal to us, as Jewish people and as Americans. In America, we are both - both the people and a nation. Of course, we are an ancient people, too ... ancient in experience and in a history that is lengthy with tales of woe and injustice. So we believe in the law, but we know that it cannot totally resolve our difficulties."

"So if the law does not always succeed, and we know that are faith remains firm, still, what is one to do? Well, we must exercise the power of our spirit. We need to communicate that our spirit remains unfazed by adversity ... that our spirit possesses sufficient power to bond the father and the child, the mother and the child, with patience and determination. Our spiritual power needs to be demonstrated, not for our sake alone, but for the sake of this wonderful nation. You know, we Jews continue to have much to teach the world."

From the audience, a man in one of the front rows stood up to shout, "They do not want us here! They want us out. There is no place for Jews."

This observation led to an avalanche of shouting. From the mezzanine, an anonymous voice yelled, "That's a lot of rot. The Irish don't despise anybody except Yankees and maybe themselves."

A few laughed.

"You can laugh," a man in the front row exclaimed, "but they despise us. Maybe they even fear us. The Irish hate the Yankees just as the Yankees hate them, but they both have no use for us. This is a goyish country. It's for goyim. There is no room for the Jews, especially when things get bad. This depression has brought out decades of hate. Second to the depression, they hate the Jews."

A woman's voice from the front row of seats filled the momentary lull. She was middle-aged with black hair tied in a bun at the back. "Mr. Newman, do you see what this violence has done to us? It has made us doubt ourselves and America, too. We are not usually this haunted by fear, but we feel alone and violated. Mr. Newman, talk sense to us, please."

Many people were frightened; many more did not know what to do. Newman could sense their feelings. Was this to be the America of their dreams - a society that looked at any person of the Jewish faith as being alien? He wanted to admit to the lady that he did not know how to help her.

However, he had orders to follow, although he had little sense of whether he had the strength within himself to lead these people in any direction. "God will help me," he thought; but then again, "if God does not help me then the way needs to be made nonetheless."

"My friends," Newman slowly attempted to regain his confidence. "My friends, the United States is no more Russia than it is Egypt. No one, no one can tell you to get out. The days of the Exodus are over. There will never be an exodus from America, because America's promise lives within each of us and in all other people who have found peace here. There is peace in the promise."

Newman sensed that the quiet he felt within himself was echoed by the quiet in the auditorium. Only the motors of the fans hummed as he rested his voice. His hands did not rest. Newman spoke with his hands as though he held a baton which he would wave before the crowd.

"Some folks in this town may have a hardened heart towards you," Newman acknowledged, "but these hardened hearts are not the strengths of these people, and they are not the strengths of this nation. We need to let these people know that our concern for going about our lives will defeat any hardened heart." Newman finished abruptly. "Allow me to work with you, so that we may present our concerns to all the people of the community. Then we shall get a sense of who we are and what this community stands for."

Mr. Joruchoff took his arm and thanked him. A group of men and women, mostly the older people in the audience, introduced themselves while asking him a multitude of questions. "Have you ever met my cousin in New York, Milton Krensky?" "New York is a large place. Not yet, anyway. Sure, I'll look him up when I get back. Your name is ...?"

Finally, Newman made his way off the stage and away from the podium. There was polite applause. A few people in the rear even stood to get a better look at him. But Newman sensed that there was skepticism in the crowd, too.

Doubt and disappointment were causing many to test Newman just as injustice had tested the notion of faith, any faith.

"Mr. Newman," an older woman said as he passed her row, "what is wrong with a miracle or two? Mr. Newman, don't you believe in miracles?"

She held on to his arm so that he could not pass until he had answered her. "My dear, Jews keep time by miracles. That's how we got to be so old ... working the miracle shift is no easy duty.

He did not return to his seat but slipped outside of the auditorium, feeling like a messenger laden with responsibilities even after his message had been delivered. He, too, longed for miracles.

Outside, he noticed how cool the evening air was without any discernible breeze. The air had dried out, and he could smell the summer aromas. Newman walked the streets, wanting to lose himself in the community. He enjoyed seeing fields of tall grasses and wildflowers. The marshes were full of cottontails, and the ocean lay beyond the marshes. Smells of ripening pear, plum, and apple trees brought him summer. "Strange," Newman thought, "that the land brings forth beauty and fruitfulness while it nurtures human hardness."

"You look like you might need some company, Mr. Newman." Suddenly there was Rebecca Collier. "Mind if I walk with you a ways?"

"You have a way of showing up, don't you?" said Jake with a trace of a smile. He was glad to see her.

There was an attractiveness about her that Newman found interesting. Her skin was radiant, and her brown eyes complimented her hair, still worn pulled back from her face. Newman observed how chiseled her features actually were, and maybe that was the reason that he caught himself looking at her. "Rebecca, company is always appreciated."

"Well, that is good, but you'll have to stop calling me Rebecca. My friends call me Beckah." She smiled and her face possessed a kind of fullness and honesty that Newman associated with youth, the beauty of youth he had simply forgotten.

"Have you ever been to the Fellsway Water Reserve? It's a chain of lakes that are in the conservation forest on the west side of town. I think they were created as an emergency water supply," Beckah continued, "but I use them as a place to take walks. From that ledge over there, you can see the marshes that lead to the sea. I love that place. It is full of birds and plants that exist as if nothing else existed in the world, and it is one of my favorite spots. Shall we take a look?"

"You lead the way."

Newman's mind was suddenly at rest. Beckah took hold of his arm as she walked him through the western part of the town, through a neighborhood he vaguely remembered. With her all the details of streets and yards and architecture came alive.

The Victorian houses were constructed of brown fieldstone or clapboards, painted with coordinating trim. Carriage houses were set off from the main houses. Even the old barns, now converted into garages, had flowers planted around their foundations. Two parks graced the west side, one even had a brook that parted the greenery down its center.

"My uncle asked my brother and me to live with him after my mother passed away," Beckah began, "so I moved here from Boston. I remember thinking that Mystic was like a village, and I couldn't wait to leave. But then I began to love the town. I felt secure in knowing the streets, and the people became like an extended family to me. My brother, David, went to California about ten years ago. He's involved in the movie-making business, something to do with advertising and promotions, and he also is involved in a winery. Doesn't that sound like California?" she laughed. Her features were sharp in an aristocratic sort of way, and her complexion was extremely fair. Even with her hair pulled back, she had so much hair she reminded him of Snow White, with her hair and her red lipstick that contrasted to her white skin. "Snow White," he said to himself.

"David wants all of us to go out to California, but that is not going to happen. My husband, Michael, has his family and his business ... anyway, I like it here. I graduated from Mystic High School and, thanks to my uncle, went to Middlesex College. My uncle and I thought the country-like atmosphere at Middlesex was right for me ... something like that." Beckah's words and expression melded into the evening air.

Lovely oak trees with enormous trunks marked each street as though nature had coordinated a landscape design with the town fathers. At places, the roots had risen above the cement sidewalks creating large cracks and bumps. This was a New England summer evening, Newman reflected. There were stars and a warm comfortableness to the evening air. Maybe it was the trees that wrapped each street in shadows that gave him a delightful feeling of serenity. He loved the interplay of shadows with skylight and the trees, for they were the treasures of New England.

"I knew Jenny well ... as well as she let herself be known," Beckah began. Newman looked at her, but did not say anything.

Beckah understood the pause for what it was. How could she tidily describe Jenny to Jake, especially someone like Jenny. "I know that you and Jenny were old friends. Long ago, anyway, you were friends and that seemed to mean something to her."

"Jenny and I grew up together. Childhood friends have a way of always being friends, as though all the years after childhood just get in the way. You know, the friendship remains suspended in time and mostly unchanged ... as though one's life is like an interruption or just a vacation. Funny, but I thought of her as a forever kind of friend, and maybe she thought the same way. I guess the present doesn't always need to peek into one's memories and demand to be recognized or paid attention to. Isn't that the way the present sometimes works, raking up the past and everything about the past? Something like that. Yes, we were friends."

Beckah listened and followed the twists and turns of Newman's words and his expressions. "Well, I knew her when she was a senior at college, and I was just thinking of going there. Even when she graduated, she worked at the college, and often I got to see her. I would see her at the school library where she worked. A whole bunch of years passed. I got married, and my family life changed my path, whatever that was. Then we met up again, and I got to know her, sort of the way two sisters get to know one another. We hit it off nicely.

Beckah provided a sense of chronology in her conversation. She had a way of explaining large periods of time that Newman knew nothing about, and she did it with broad, sweeping strokes of memory. Newman began to assemble some of these impressions - the threads of Jenny's life, some of the particulars that went into shaping her life beyond the fact of her death, because it was her life that mattered to him. It appeared to Newman that he was grasping for fragments of some still unknown jigsaw puzzle - Jenny's life and her death, and in his mind Newman sought to get close to her.

Beckah offered little as to why or what may have precipitated Jenny's suicide. While the idea of committing suicide struck Newman as wrong, he required an answer. Unmarried, lonely, anguished ... weren't these just stereotypes that explained very little about Jenny? At best, weren't these reasons just old wives' tales that the grieving family and society could use to provide a "comfort factor" for everybody else.

This may be the usual way untimely deaths are recalled, but Newman found little in the way of useful insights from such talk

"Did you ever suspect she might take her life?" Newman questioned.

"I never thought about it until she did. She was unpredictable, but she wasn't anything more than that. She wasn't dangerous or anything like that. Really, I felt she was remarkably sure of herself. I thought of Jenny as self-contained, if you know what I mean. I thought she was quite pretty, but I can't say she did much to herself. She dressed simply, but it fit her, unassuming and innocent-like. I suppose she had what some would describe as a long nose. You know, a Jewish nose, but I liked it. I thought that it fit her, and it gave her a great sense of who she was. But she may not have shared that idea; noses are personal."

There was something wry about Beckah's remarks. Maybe she was self-conscious, but this surprised Newman. Why? Was Beckah just being realistic or astute or merely caring? Newman took it no further than this, but he wondered about what other depths of introspection distinguished this lady.

"Her nose?" questioned Newman, catching up to the conversation. "I never gave much thought to it. She looked fine to me."

"To me, too, and to others, since there were men in her life. In fact, there were a number of men I wanted to introduce her to. When I had parties, Jenny frequently came by, but I can't say that I knew much about her social life. I know she was interested in politics, that she wrote letters to the State Department and to the President ... usually about Jewish relief or assistance for people wishing to enter the United States or something of that nature. But that is not exactly the same as knowing her ... knowing what her days were like or something like that."

"Two or three years ago, I did notice some definite changes in her behavior, some odd type of changes. She became terribly alienated with her work at the college. She seemed to detest many of the people she worked with in the

84

library, though not everybody. I remember her telling me that she did respect certain people, but a whole lot of others, especially among the faculty, were hardly her favorites. Most of the problems were about the war in Europe and what the United States should do to help people who were being arrested by the Germans or Fascist governments that cooperated with the Nazis. Reports about roundups of Jewish families and what not set her off. Anytime a story appeared in the newspapers or perhaps from a speaker she may have heard, she became livid. She was quite the letter writer. She even blasted President Roosevelt and Eleanor Roosevelt, which was unusual because Jenny had worked for the Roosevelt committee in town. But when she heard the reports coming out of Europe ... the assaults on Jews walking in the streets, the destruction of property, and the fact that people were fleeing for their lives, that made her act like a crazy person."

"She became ... eccentric. Almost no one who worked with her in the Sunday school felt comfortable with her any longer, and there was even talk about preventing her from working with the children."

"She kept talking about how the children needed to be instructed to understand who they were. She said that the children had been exposed to bad role models in their lives, and those included their parents and even the people who ran the Sunday school. She said that the community was full of 'idolaters'. That was her word, 'idolaters'. She was adamant, saying, 'The idolaters had won. People thought they were free, but how could people be free if Jews in Germany feared for their safety? Why weren't all Jews outraged? The children will be the biggest losers,' Beckah quoted Jenny, 'and the President should be doing something to save the children.'"

"This didn't sit well with a lot of people, especially those who didn't want anything to do with getting into a war. That included the people who ran the Religious School."

"Jenny made no bones about it. She would say that the Religious School was in league with those who had become unconcerned about the values of the children. Jewish people were being duped," Beckah explained. "That was the way she put it. 'Caution ruled; even worse, money and caution ruled. The idolators had prevailed.'"

"And she didn't let up. Every time I saw her she looked more and more tired or worn. She had been attending lectures in Boston, the Conrad Hall Lecture Series. When an envoy from a German trade group, or some government representative, was invited to give a talk about how Germany was defending the people of Europe from communism and the international Jewish conspiracy, Jenny became so irate that she demonstrated outside the auditorium. She then went inside and ended up getting herself locked up in a Boston jail cell for the evening. I went down and bailed her out, and it was odd to see this elf of a person become so adamant. She spurned a lot of people and found herself the butt of many jokes. But she kept talking, writing letters, carrying picket signs, and generally finding herself further and further at odds with people in the community, people who basically wanted no waves. It was more than politics. It was everything."

Beckah continued, "Her world was a great deal different than mine, and I did not get to know her well until I started teaching at the Religious School. That was six or six and a half years ago. That's when we became friends, the way people who work together often become friends. We had lunch, maybe an occasional cup of coffee after school let out. I felt comfortable with her, and she made me laugh. Jenny was witty; she was funny in the way she was able to capture the essence of a person, and she loved the children. Sometimes when I was unsure as to how to tell a parent or a student that something was not quite right, Jenny had a little phrase or a quip which made me see what a house of cards every school actually is. When a student couldn't graduate in the

Spring, she'd just say to the child, 'Don't worry. We have two graduations, one in the Spring and one in the Summer.' Or if a child was having difficulty and was thinking about dropping one of the classes, she would sit down and convince the student to take the dreaded class at a later time. Maybe Jenny just understood kids in a way that a parent doesn't."

"Even at the college, she had spent a lot of time with students, especially as a volunteer to student groups. She gave them all the responsibility and all the time that they needed to get done whatever it was they were doing. I admired her energy, and her sense of priorities."

Newman looked more amazed and asked, "But why did she take her own life? That's what I still do not understand."

"I don't know. She wasn't the kind of person who just backed down from problems or from anything else. She cared about people, that was for sure."

Beckah was not finished, though Newman saw a certain strained quality come over her face. "Look, people would tell me that they'd see her walking about the town at all hours of the day and in all kinds of weather. I guess she had lived in a part of a house that was owned by an old man who was close to her. When he died, the house was sold. She had mentioned that to me ... how much her life changed when, I think his name was Mr. Harland, died. It was like a chapter in her life had ended. She had only nice things to say about him. In fact she had taken to writing down either a story or something about him. Anyway, when he died, she had to move; so, she rented a third-floor attic apartment on the other side of the Square. She had so many stairs to climb that she asked me to take her bicycle, an old English Raleigh, which is still in my garage. She never used that bike again."

"I began to notice that she often carried on conversations with herself. She had always been on the thin side, but over the last year before she died, she grew scrawny. She was becoming more and more detached. I can't say that a whole lot of people looked at her as anything but odd, beyond the pale, if you know what I mean.

Newman listened with concentration, weighing Beckah's words and adjusting the images of her words to some level of knowing a person at one point in their life and relating that to another point in time. Beckah's words were softly spoken; they were gently stated and revealed a sensitive ear and eye which Newman admired. Beckah provided glimpses of Jenny that her stories helped him to recall - the image of a young girl who wanted life to be an exchange of ideas, constructive, illuminating, in search of a sensibility that connected the world to herself. Newman knew that he never loved Jenny, but he loved the kind of person she was. He remembered her on her bicycle as a child, a picture in his mind that he had never forgotten.

"There were times when I saw her with her mother, and the two of them looked so frail. Jenny appeared tired and beaten down, as though she had been ill. Despite their differences in age, Jenny didn't look all that much younger than her mother. Some of the children called them 'the sisters of the Square.'"

"But an image does stand out in my mind, and that's how tiny Jenny appeared. When she walked with her mother, it was as if a child were accompanying her mother. They walked slowly, burdened by the shopping bags they carried, each one holding a large bag in either hand. God knows what they were buying."

"When I first met her, she was always dressed well and was as bright as bright could be. She was the first to read the Sunday Times, which she carried under her arm to and from Sunday school, and she talked about books and plays. But over the last year she'd refer to all such things as 'idolatry'. I guess she was referring to the fascination with clothes or cars or what one wanted to do with one's life. Idolatry, that is what she called it.

"I thought you'd want to know this. Once, maybe one of

the first times I met her, we were talking, and she mentioned her childhood, growing up and all. She even mentioned your name. She had been talking about interesting people she had grown up with, and your name came up. She was proud to say that the two of you had been close for a time and that you were a good person. 'Quite, quite a friend ... a true friend,' that was it."

"She was nice. More than nice, she was lovely really. Even as a child, she was eager to do the right thing, to have a sense of the world. You know, to live correctly." Newman didn't wish to take his thoughts further. His mind was busy trying to get a hold on Beckah's account.

"Doesn't it seem that she had some kind of breakdown?" Newman questioned aloud. "How else does one explain such transformations? Could there have been something physical that made a vibrant person all but bizarre or a shell of herself? Her mother must have realized all was not well. Why didn't she do something?"

"A lot of people think that, especially now that she is gone."

Beckah walked a bit and picked up a flat paving stone, a tiny paving stone and tossed it across thewater's surface and easily made it skim on top of the clear water.

"For almost a year, before she became reclusive and withdrawn, she was part of a campaign to stop buying German-made goods. She picketed the various jewelry stores in town and the Grand Marsh Department Store. That was a bitter · time around here, because the stores were doing poorly to begin with and picketers hurt business even more."

"Jenny was one of the soldiers of the movement to make people realize that the treatment the Jewish people in Germany were receiving was outrageous and the only way to make the German government hear that message was through a boycott of their goods and a boycott of stores that sold such things. A lot of merchants were upset. It sure started an argument in my house and in lots of other places, too."

Beckah ran her fingers through her hair. Her memories agitated her, the way something forgotten but troublesome bedevils us when it is recalled. But she continued to flesh out her point.

"If anything, Jenny felt defeated by the lack of support. It was bad enough for most people to make it through hard economic times. Jobs were impossible to come by, but Jenny kept parading outside the stores. Her signs accused Germany of anti-Semitism. The shops that sold Italian shoes or Spanish handbags, and even the Jewish stores, had Jenny picketing outside their windows.

"She was doing what she had to do. That is what I thought, but Michael and many others objected to public displays like that. They thought that Jenny was a kook that made problems worse." Beckah's voice trailed a bit and her mind was somewhat tired.

"You don't have to go on," Newman said with a quiet voice that surprised himself in its whisper.

"I just want you to know that she was someone who tried to wake people up. After that, she just seemed to get further away from people. She had become a shell of the person that I and others had known. She was bizarre, I reluctantly say that. Maybe she was sick, maybe she was just coming apart. I saw her as a victim. Whatever it was that may have brought it on, she was not the person I thought I knew."

"I began to wonder. So many people around here said she was out of her mind and could not be held accountable for what she did. But I felt that what she did, taking her life, was like the Jenny I originally knew - a person with standards who understood a bit about herself."

Newman listened to all of Beckah's impressions and insights. He realized that although Jenny was not the reason he found himself in Mystic, her plight was part of the problem that directed him to the town. The decision to die, Jenny's decision, was an admission of hopelessness. That was clear to Newman, and it was the only way that her death was understandable to him. But he objected to anybody being led in such a direction, or driven there, or for whatever reason made to feel that there was no sense in living.

"She sounds like a refugee ... or that her mind or her heart had been made to see only futility. But she grew up in this town. Why did she possess such a perspective, such a vision? What did she know or thought she knew that we do not?" Newman thought aloud.

"That must be it," Newman caught himself. "She was a refugee but not of a place. She was like an outcast, but one who wished to be an outcast, almost needed to be. Who wants to join the idolaters?" Newman's brain churned but little else made any sense.

$$*****************************$$

Beckah and Newman had come to a forested area. In the sky was the speckled glimmer of the night's first stars and a half moon. Together, they continued in silence down a wide path which led to a pond, a pond which was rather large and broad and perched as if on a plateau five or six feet above the rest of the land. The rise was gradual and pleasing to the eye, and bushes and saplings were everywhere near it banks.

Here, near the water, the air was cool. In the twilight there was both quiet and serenity. This was a country place, but it was close to any number of cities and towns. Even Boston was just a few minutes from the pond, although there was no suggestion of people any- where nearby.

"This has always been one of my favorite places. I don't think I've ever been to this spot and felt sad or worried about whatever was happening in my life ... at least for a while," Beckah said. As she spoke, she took off her shoes, sandals actually, and walked over to the edge of the water.

"Over there," she pointed, "is an even larger pond, but this one is my favorite. I love that little island out there.

Sometimes I think it would be wonderful to build a house on an island like that. Well, it doesn't have to be a house, just a cottage or a tiny cape. Even in winter, when the leaves are down and the pond is frozen solid, that image of a tiny house is something I find hard to resist. I told you this is a special place for me." Beckah laughed a bit and so did Jake.

"I've imagined living out there," she pointed.

"I can see that. I guess you'd need a wood stove in the winter, wouldn't you?" Newman quipped.

"Sure, what's a winter cottage without a train of smoke coming from the chimney," Beckah answered. "Don't start getting my dreams all complicated ... stoves, a hearth, and all that. Pretty soon you'll want to know where I intend to pick up the groceries. Then all the complexities of civilization start to creep back into the picture! I just want my cottage to be a picture, uncomplicated, and nice and easy. Just a nice and easy place." And it sounded as though all the little joking was now gone from Beckah's voice.

Newman's mind was pleased to look out over the water and to the trees and forested embankment beyond the water's edge. Reflections of the moon lay upon the water, quite still except for an imperceptible ripple. Deliberately, he cleared his mind. He placed his socks and shoes by the shore and waded into the water which felt cold but soothing.

"There must be an underground stream that feeds the lakes," he told himself, the chilling water making his toes somewhat numb.

Beckah and Newman said little, their feet splashing water neatly around their submerged ankles. Each was more intent on walking in the water than in continuing their talk. Maybe it was their conversation, maybe it was the gentleness of Beckah's personality that made Newman glad to be in her company.

"Did I ask you what you were doing at the meeting this evening?" Newman asked. "Somehow I got the feeling that this is charity work for you."

"Jake, I grew up as poor as poor can be. I don't think I have lost track of who I am. My husband's money hasn't been able to blot out what my life was like. But you were a friend of Jenny's so I kind of felt responsible for you ... sort of like a guest."

"Well, don't get me wrong. I'm glad you showed up."

"I'm glad, too."

They walked back to the center of town. There was a slowness to their gait, as though the walk was an end unto itself. They got along easily and intuitively, so much so that Newman had all but forgotten that he hardly knew her or anything about her.

He never said anything to himself, but if he had it would have been that this person was unusual. So many things had become unusual to him, it was a wonder that he remembered that he was there, in this town, for a purpose that had little to do with him, his past, or anything else associated with his likes or dislikes.

Suddenly remembering, he ordered himself, "You're here to do your job. Do your job. Everything is secondary at best, but first do your job."

"Thanks for the tour," Jake said as they came to the center of the Square.

"No thanks is needed. I'm usually around the Square for one thing or another. I'll be checking in on you." Beckah laughed at this and just as mysteriously as she appeared, she was gone.

"I should have walked her to her house," Newman thought to himself. "How dumb."

But it was too late for that. With more nervous energy than he knew what to do with, Newman continued to walk through the many neighborhoods of the town.

"Home," he thought.

He realized suddenly that he could not go back to the hotel without first stopping by the shiva house, the house of mourning, Jenny's house. He knew that this visit would be difficult.

****

The house was one of the two-family houses on Belmont Hill, an old-time Yankee neighborhood, which was now mostly Irish with a sprinkling of Jewish families. Mr. Glass had had a small dress factory on the outskirts of Suffolk Square.

Mr. Glass had died when Jenny was in junior high school. Jake remembered what a sad day that had been for Jenny. Newman remembered walking with her after the funeral through a wooded reservation area filled with paths and streams. Sitting on the ground, Jake had felt a tear drop from Jenny's eyes onto his hand. Then there were more tears. Newman shared them all.

Jenny was an only child, but Mrs. Glass did have some other relatives in the town. Newman had thought Mrs. Glass would move away when her husband passed away, but she never did. Newman remembered her saying, "I never wanted to live in this place, but my husband liked it. The people are nice, he would say. They were `special' to him. I'm too old to move now. This is `home' to my family. A family needs to be rooted," she often said when Jake visited the house. "That's the job of parents. That's my job anyway ... to have a home ready for my family."

Newman wanted to see Mrs. Glass. He wanted her to remember him just as he wished to remember Jenny. Wooden steps, worn by foot traffic, led to the second- floor doorway. The carpeted hallway with a thin, tall table at the entrance-way looked familiar to Newman. The green floral wallpaper looked bright and cheerful and new. It had been years since he had been in this hallway, but the feel of the place was familiar and comforting.

Since crowds of people were paying their respects, getting into the second-floor apartment meant sliding through people-packed rooms. A table laden with cakes, urns of coffee, tea and bottles of seltzer water made the dining room particularly crowded. Children darted between groups of adults.

94

A large, screened porch just beyond the living room was crowded, too. Bridge chairs were everywhere. Every window had been raised so that a refreshing breeze made its way through the apartment. The outside air had become dry.

Newman knew no one, but people smiled at him, probably believing him to be a cousin or some person that had worked with someone in the family. "Take something to eat," an elderly lady remarked to him. "Eat something. There is iced coffee in the kitchen." She then disappeared.

In the kitchen Mrs. Glass sat on a kitchen chair. Newman joined the host of mourners standing in front of her. When he reached her, Jake realized that she had no idea who he was. She looked at him, trying to discern something familiar about his face. She was silent. Some moments passed. Mrs. Glass looked harder, more intently, looking to remember. "Jake Newman, it is you. Jake?"

"It is me, Mrs. Glass."

"Jake Newman. Jake, you know about my Jenny?"

"I'm sorry, Mrs. Glass."

She said nothing else. She looked at Newman as though she wished she could hold back the news. She tried to protect Newman with her eyes, but she could not protect him. Her heart was too torn.

As her eyes explored Newman's eyes, he shared her pain. It was the pain of remembering his youth and Jenny's youth. It was the pain of recalling that quiet smile, that shyness of spirit that was gone.

And Mrs. Glass knew, too, that Jenny was no more. Her child was no more. Jake's sorrow proved to Mrs. Glass that Jenny was gone. "Jake. Jake. You came back to see Jenny." she moaned. "They took my Jenny from me. Jake, they took my Jenny." Mrs. Glass' eyes cried to Jake a most personal cry, soft and silent, full of the emptiness of life that comes with death.

Jakes's heart was filled with tears, and his eyes were clouded over with sorrow. It was a sorrow he had known but struggled not to know or admit. It was a sadness he would never be able to forget. It was a pain that would return each time a sadness gripped him, each time a rip jolted his being, dizzying his eyes and making him tumble into a pain that only waited to echo through his mind.

Jake's eyes filled with tears, enormous soulful tears. 'They took my Jenny from me,' reverberated in his head, a cry, the kind of cry that perhaps only a mother can release upon the earth. The world was battling against darkness, and that darkness seized a mother's child. And Newman understood the cry for what it was - an expression of pain, an awful pain signalling a victory for all the foulness within the world. Newman's face was stilled by the victory of evil, while he swore some expression of revenge.

More people made their way into the kitchen, forcing those already in the room out one door or another. Jake and Mrs. Glass could not look at each other any longer. They held out their hands to one another, and Jake whispered, "Goodbye," before he made his way to the living room and outside. He made no further effort to see Mrs. Glass.

Chapter Six

Keys of the Olivetti

At dawn he returned to his hotel. He slept until noon, finding comfort and familiarity in the breezy room. For the greater part of the week, Newman's time was spent talking to people in the town. Often, people would stop him in his walks and introduce themselves to him. He was becoming known, almost as well known as if he had spent his whole life in the Square. Newman listened to the shopkeepers, to the ladies who carried their bundles to and from their daily shopping routines. Sometimes he spent his day at the city hall, the district court, or with an alderman fleshing out how a New England town lived in that summer of 1941.

Everyday, too, he took out his Olivetti typewriter and began pecking at the keyboard. Only through writing, Newman told himself, could he explain how, for a moment, an American community bordered on a pogrom. In his mind, Newman was not sure what was the more important question. Was it more important to ask why this place found its peace briefly shattered or why nearly everyone now sought to forget that anything unusual had occurred? Newman searched the keys of the Olivetti for an answer.

****

Newman dressed in a dark grey suit that was maybe a little too dark for a summer party. But it was the only suit he owned that was a bit more formal than everyday wear. With a starched white shirt and a blue-striped tie, Newman believed that he was prepared for the Collier's engagement party. More than a few individuals were envious that he and not they had been invited.

"You must rate highly, Mr. Newman," Mr. Ginsburg kidded him. "I get few invitations from the wealthiest members of the community. My wife tells me it is doubtless due to the fact that she has little to wear," Ginsburg continued in his humorous style.

"Is that the case, Mr. Ginsburg?" Newman questioned,

still encouraging the good-natured fellow.

"Only if you believe that two stores of clothing are insufficient. Anyway, considering that so many people have hardly enough bread, clothes is less a compelling reason than my wife lets on. The truth is that we go to bed quite early, everyday, and parties begin too late in the evening for my wife and for me. But you are a young fellow, and you belong at such an affair!"

"You are a kind fellow, and I shall tell your wife exactly that. But I plan on making this an early evening, too," Newman confided to the insightful hotel manager.

In little more than forty minutes, the cab dropped Newman off at a long, circular driveway leading to an enormous, rambling shingled house. Four stories in height, the house exhibited Romanesque arches and wide porches that only added to the size of the house.

Cars were parked on either side of the driveway, and some were parked on a lawn area, too, which revealed two tennis courts and a huge, close-cropped grassy knoll that made up the backyard. Newman noticed that the house sat atop a small rocky ledge, and it was difficult not to be quite taken by this New England masterpiece.

Two large and quite wide front doors were swung open by similarly dressed teenage boys that led to a crowded room of white tuxedoed men and elegantly dressed women, sparkling in light-colored dresses and glimmering in a room filled with waiters, fine furnishings, and a staircase from a movie set.

"Depression? What depression," Newman asked himself. Remembering his attire, Newman remained distinctly visible in a sea of after-dinner wear.

"Don't you love cozy little parties," Newman said to a waiter while seizing a passing glass of champagne.

"Welcome," a man's voice rang out making Newman turn completely around. "I'm Michael Collier."

"Jake Newman. Thank you for the invitation. Cheers and congratulations!"

"Have you met my daughter?" Michael asked but did not wait for an answer before he quickly moved between a number of people shouting, "Sarah ... Sarah ... over here. I want you to meet someone."

A small retinue of individuals had assembled, and Michael made the introductions. "This is my daughter, Sarah, the bride-to-be." She looked very much like the bride-to-be. Her face beamed with a smile. Tall, almost willowy, with large brown eyes, a gracious shaped face, and long blonde hair, she looked the epitome of youth. This is youth, Newman thought.

"Congratulations. Your parents were kind enough to invite me, and just seeing you makes me glad I came. I hope that will always be as happy as you look right now."

"Thank you. We're quite excited. It's hard for me to believe that this is happening to me. All these people ... engaged ... I'm about as happy as I am nervous. Well, I'm glad to meet you. Have you met Allen? You probably haven't, have you?" Sarah asked. Reaching into a passing crowd of people, she seized a hand. But the hand she held took her into the crowd.

Michael moved back into the conversation, having gone from one group to another in a socializing sort of way. He and a tall, rather thin lad suddenly appeared in front of Newman. Sarah quickly joined the group, too.

"Allen Golden, please meet Mr. Jake Newman." Newman replied, "Jake Newman. How do you do? Best of luck to you."

"Nice to meet you. Thank you." Allen's voice was as youthful as the shade of embarrassment that reddened his face, a thin face with large cheekbones and a pronounced Adam's apple.

Holding one another's arm, Sarah and Allen looked like youth itself. Newman could not help smiling and thinking about the naturalness of starting out in life, the optimism of a world that seems to be caught in time. Here was a couple twirling before his eyes with a house, no an estate, filled with guests and the world beaming in approval. Newman liked that. He liked happy stories, stories that foretold a happy tale. And he enjoyed seeing such a story, especially in youth.

"You look as though you are a member of the family, Mr. Newman," a raspy voice made Newman look around.

"Forgive me. I'm Jessica Borgass. You're our New York connection, aren't you?"

Newman thought that the voice fit the tiny woman, who was dressed in a long, black dress, and looking at him with a broad smile and enormous green eyes. A cigarette dangled from her fingers. Only then did Newman realize that this lady was as thin and gaunt- looking as the white-papered cigarette.

"Miss Borgass?"

"Mrs. Borgass. My husband is over there. There, the little rolly-polly guy; there, that's Alvin. He and Michael are in the insurance business. He's one of Michael's partners, one of a dozen or so." Her voice nearly droned in a low, nasal tone.

"I'm Jake Newman." He said this unconsciously, until he caught himself. "But you know that."

"Yes, Michael pointed you out. And I know you're here to write about what happened in Suffolk Square."

This caught Newman by surprise. "How did you know I plan on writing about this?"

"Mr. Newman, this is New England not Zanzibar. We get all kinds of newspapers in Massachusetts, you know? I've seen your name a number of times. You did a story on Detroit about a year ago. And two or three years ago, you wrote about school children in Atlanta, I believe."

"You have a good memory, Mrs. Borgass. A very good memory. But I am mostly an observer. I'm more concerned that the people I get to meet find me useful, though being useful is incredibly difficult. The reporting and the stories are reminders of what happened, what worked or failed or otherwise got people over some difficult times. What was useful."

Newman began to wonder if the lady's voice was beginning to rub off on him, for his voice had become dried and gasping for air.

"Well, this town has little in the way of problems. A fluke occurred ... just a fluke, but no real problems. You know what I mean?"

"Sure."

"Well, look that is up to you. All I know is that this town is doing fine. Little slips here and there, perhaps. Nice crowd, huh?" Mrs. Borgass boasted.

Newman nodded but not before a waiter carrying an enormous tray of champagne glasses made a pass by him, and again Newman swiftly took a glass of champagne from the gleaming silver tray.

"You must like this town," Newman volunteered.

Mrs. Borgass laughed. "I guess I do. Sometimes I ask myself why I didn't go someplace else. But this place is excellent and close to Boston, and it is quite hard to leave Boston. To be frank, at this point in my life I almost do not care. But I am not without some advice for you."

"As long as it is free, I'm happy to listen."

"My advice is to do your business and head on out of here. Peace and prosperity are what make this town operate, and that is the bottom line. One more thing; in New England, only success is remembered. Everything else fades and is fast forgotten. Do you know how desperately some people want to be successful? These people are like that. They desire success about as much as they do anything. It is the oxygen of their existence." Mrs. Borgass then moved into the crowd of other guests, and Newman saw her only one other time before the evening ended.

Success, he thought. The desire to be successful over everything else in one's path. Newman understood that need.

****

Winter 1928 ...

"The Inspector knows that a boatload of guns and refugees will be approaching the harbor in ten days." The old man's wife could hold an audience just as the old man had captured Newman's attention.

Sitting in the back of a coffee shop on one of the busiest streets in the port of Haifa, Newman saw his pal Spinney break open a bag full of loaves of Middle Eastern bread. Spinney spotted Newman and signalled, "Want some of this?"

Newman shook his head. He was hungry, but he was more interested in the sight of a roomful of twenty young men and women, all of whom were Western or European in appearance. Some of the women looked as though they were clerks in department stores or secretaries. The men were more coarsely dressed. They looked out of place in a British colony where uniforms helped distinguish local people from police or British officials. There was a refugee quality to the faces of these fellows. Some were pale; others were burned by the sun. All looked unlike the Arab-dressed men and women and the German-speaking population that made up the mainstay of Haifa's population.

Again, Spinney signalled Newman. This time, receiving no answer, he took his loaves of bread over to him. "Your friend is going to get us arrested. You know that, don't you? The British police lack a sense of humor about smuggling guns into Palestine, and we should take our asses out of here." Spinney continued eating.

"She asked me to come. What could I say? The old man would have wanted me to help. Anything she does doesn't surprise me. Whatever she's up to - guns, murder - she's a tough old lady. Simon, the old man, was the same way. He meant business."

Spinney remained unconvinced of any obligation to anyone and did not mince words about it. "Lovely people these gun-runners, but we are not in the same line of work. Forgive me for saying so, but this has nothing to do with us. Really, why kick ass about their problems? Being of the Irish persuasion, I can verify that the British are without scruples. They will burst right through that door and send us to a most uncomfortable prison in the hottest desert. It is part of their fixation with stepping on people that makes me know this."

"I can't stay out it, Jim, but you can. Go ahead. Get your ass out of here before it's too late. Really, you take off."

Jim stayed, and Newman knew why he was staying. They had been childhood friends. Spinney was not one to look for danger, but loyalty was a weighty consideration to him.

Talking about guns in foreign ports was a subject merchant marines were instructed to avoid. "Get yourself into that shit and don't expect any kind of bail out," had been the advice of more than one ship officer.

Newman listened to the old lady's conversation, anxious to know where the guns were to be dropped off. She conferred with two men. One wore green gardening pants, with lightweight rubber boat shoes, perforated for coolness. He was red complexioned with a large, clean-shaven face and enormous ears. In his shirt pocket were eyeglasses, neatly folded. This man, Myron by name, was a consequential member of Gerda's group. "Myron would like your attention," was Gerda's way of introducing him, and that normally made for a responsive audience.

Although Myron was five feet, eight inches tall, the second member of the group towered over both him and Gerda. This man, Sydney, had a British accent that struck Newman as odd. He wore thick glasses, and his blond hair was neatly parted and combed; his face reminded Newman of a minister or clerk. Newman thought that Sydney could well be a businessman or a government official. In fact, Sydney was a go-between for those individuals who profited in a multi-faceted smuggling trade that involved prospective clients such as Myron and Gerda. It was obvious that they knew one another, which was evident by the familiarity they exhibited. Newman learned that the transfer of guns would occur about a mile off the rather rough seas north of Haifa. A fisherman would provide his boat for the pick up.

"British patrols off the coast are lax, but the British understand the cost of operations. They wish to intercept guns or ammunition on land where an array of informants can be utilized," Sydney explained. "The British want to make sure the Arab religious and tribal leaders are happy."

Gerda nodded. Then Myron interjected his voice into the discussion. "It's our job to make everybody less than happy. It's our job to get as many guns in the hands of our people as we can. More guns, more Jewish emigres. That's the equation. The more Jews with guns, the better. That is a bonus. Do not waste the opportunity to save either people or guns, for the movement needs both. May God go with you."

Soon all but Gerda, Jim, and Newman had left. "Will you boys help us?" the old woman asked. "One of the people on that boat is important to us. He is from France, a Monsieur Rosenthal. He has many connections for our movement. I only ask that you help get him here safely, so that our work can continue. Will you help? Myron and I have a plan, a diversion that we believe may bring us success. May we explain it to you?"

Chapter Seven

Mr. and Mrs. Simon

The Highest Window

From the highest window, the world seems so
   alive.
Summer birds play their little games,
Bound up in the trees, bound up in the sky,
Way up in the air, no one cares, my life is
   passing by.

From the highest window, no one bothers
   to look,
Just a place to watch the wind play hide and
   seek, just a place to dream and write.
From this highest window, a place to spend my
   life.

Who can say? Maybe someday I'll find someone
who can share this view with me.

Someone who feels about the wind and the
   leaves and the trees,
Someone who can love me.

When will I know that I am alive, when will
   that ever be?
Or from the highest window, will this be life
   for me?

Someone who cares for me.
There must be that someone.
From the highest window,
   that is where I'll be,
Listening for your love,
   waiting on every breeze.

From the highest window, I can dream of you,
And no one really cares, no one really
  minds.

Way up in the sky, my life is passing by.
Only love can save me.

Love. Listening for your love.
Catch me, I'm falling.
  From the highest window
  From the highest window
From the highest window, only love can make me
  free,
Only love can make me free.

* * * * * * * * * *

By three in the afternoon, the perspiration began to build up on Newman's chest and make its way around his waist. He slipped into the bathtub to soak. He had an hour to get ready for his meeting with Beckah. He knew that the community would take a couple of days to get the word out that a man from New York was in town, to learn the purpose of his presence, and to speculate how, if at all, his presence would make a difference in the community.

Newman's thoughts turned to the meeting. He had realized that the people who listened to him probably expected little in the way of change. That was not unusual. Rightly so. Little by way of change ever occurred, Newman reasoned.

Here he was, a guy from New York, from this OAHA. What did he know of these people or their problems? "That is what most people are thinking," Newman imagined. "Do I remind them of their conscience? Am I the embodiment of their memory? No. It's as though they blame the messenger for the bad news," Newman chuckled. "They think that as soon as I get out of town, they can get on with their lives."

Finished with his bath, Newman ran his hands over his neck and looked out the window overlooking the Square. He stared down at the shops with their signs advertising Kosher products or boasting of their proprietor's name and the length of time that the business had been in existence. "These folks think I'm going to mess up their lives," he reflected. He lifted the window and opened the door, hoping to get whatever breeze might be passing by. "They fear the consequences of being heard. That must be a part of what bothers them," he realized. "They're afraid I'm going to disturb their businesses. Getting the Jews out of Egypt was probably like this. Lots of energy on the consequences. I need a miracle, too!"

"You are Mr. Newman?" A low, hollow voice came from a tall, extremely pale-faced man wearing dark- framed eyeglasses.

"I am. And you?"

"Sir, forgive me. I was just about to knock on your door. Mr. Ginsburg thought you might be in. My name is John Stinson. I am an aid to Mayor Converse, Eugene Converse, the Mayor of Mystic. The Mayor would like to extend an invitation to meet with him at his office."

The heat was obviously a bit much for the fellow. Sweat beaded on his forehead, leading to the removal of his glasses, and two or three enormous wipes of his face and neck. In a white shirt and a light-blue corduroy suit, Newman closed the door to his room and waved the gentleman to follow him downstairs to the lobby. There they were seated and with a glass of ginger ale from Mr. Ginsburg, Stinson appeared less victimized by the weather.

"I looked for you the other evening after the meeting at the theatre, but you seemed to disappear. Mayor Converse received a letter from the Organization ... of something."

"The Organization of American Hebrew Aid."

"Right. Exactly. From your director, telling of your interest in our town and requesting our cooperation. Copies of the letter were sent to the press and to the entire congressional delegation of our state. Well, the Mayor surely wants to meet you and provide whatever assistance you may require." Stinson was a polished and diplomatic fellow, and there was a genuineness to his voice that appealed to Newman.

"Mr. Stinson, our interest in this town revolves around your citizens getting beaten on the head. Their safety has obviously come into question. Mayor Converse, I am sure, does not condone such actions, but why this event occurred is perplexing. Is there something wrong with this place that the casual observer hasn't noticed?" Newman spoke in a soft voice and the activities of the lobby only served to focus his remarks. It was hard for Newman to tell if Stinson desired such bluntness, but little in Stinson's demeanor reflected irritation.

Stinson accepted his cue when Newman's voice revealed his remarks were at an end. "Clearly, the town does not sponsor chaos or public disorder, and besides this community has held an open door to whomever wished to settle here. The record is exactly that. But we have our problems, and most of it has to do with liquor and vice, the staples of most community problems. Nothing extraordinary, though."

"You know, that is probably true, but did you know that I grew up in this town a ways back? And the place remarkably has not changed. The Irish live in the same basic areas; the Italians have their little spots; the Black people are in the same few streets and so are the Jews. The place has stayed quite the same, except for those individuals who have moved up in life or simply moved on." Newman focused his attention in a sharp, pointed direction, and these words made Stinson listen with some attention. "In fact, what is odd is that so little has changed. The poor remain the poor; the ghetto remains a ghetto. In fact, there are several ghettos, except for the lovely old houses in the older part of town, the more exclusive, more pedigree part of town. Seems to me that there is something stultifying about that, if you follow? I bet that had I spent my life here I'd be in one of those ghettos right now, and the Mayor would not ask if all were well or not."

Stinson finished his drink and placed the glass on the table just to his right. "Who can say, Mr. Newman? The poor are poor and that is what the good book tells us. But no one is responsible for that, save themselves. The Mayor will be interested in meeting you. Do you think you could stop by his office in the next couple of days? It would be appreciated." Stinson had enough of the conversation, as if it were all beyond the duties he needed to perform, and now wished to disengage.

"I will stop by ... say tomorrow in the afternoon. Good enough?"

"Fine ... that will be fine. Till then. Pleasure to meet you." Newman had not realized that Stinson had placed a broad, straw hat by his side, but now placed it on his head and gave a brief wave as he left the lobby.

****

Newman entered Sher's, a delicatessen on the edge of the Square. It was a long and narrow restaurant that had tiny lamps hung along its corridor-like room. To the left side of the entrance were glimmering cases which displayed the day's prepared dishes and that reminded Newman of delicatessens in New York.

Despite the fact that the restaurant was nearly full, Newman spotted Beckah Collier. Beckah's features appeared even more pronounced in the daylight. The shape of her face was exquisite; every angle was finely wrought as a delicate piece of sculpture or perhaps glass. Now, her skin color was almost ivory white while strong reddish highlights emerged from her hair. Her hair was tied back as it was the previous evening. Her eyes were quite large and dark, and she seemed to see Newman as soon as he saw her.

"We must have similar schedules," Newman said.

"Indeed. I suspected that you eat regularly and that this would be the perfect spot." Only then did Newman notice that she was with someone.

"Glad to see you again, Mr. Newman," Michael spoke slowly and carefully.

Collier was about six feet tall, and he had dark skin, naturally so. His face had a sharpness about his nose and his chin. He was quite thin in the face, too, Newman thought. Well-dressed and groomed, Collier possessed a sense of purpose about him. Newman guessed that this was not going to be a casual meeting.

"I bet you're hungry. This place does a number of things real well. You're going to get something, aren't you Rebecca?" She nodded and Michael studied the menu with added concentration.

Newman looked at the menu, but his eyes quickly moved to one of the display cases, and he decided that it contained what he wanted. It was necessary to go to the counter and order. Newman ordered first, selecting lox, cream cheese, whitefish, and smoked mackerel. It wasn't until he sat down that he realized that this was a Kosher delicatessen which only carried dairy products. No meat was offered. A sink area, at the rear of the dining room, was open to everyone for prayers before eating. Beckah and Michael both ordered noodle pudding and a salad which they shared. Michael also ordered a sandwich of smoked sable fish. I could live on this kind of food, Newman thought. Food from the sea was Newman's favorite, despite the hefty amount of salt in such fare. Meat was rare for Newman to either order or even have a craving for, and this became the rule the older he became.

Michael worked at his food with energy, and fortunately there was plenty of it. "Mr. Newman," he began with few words by way of introduction, "society has been a faint-hearted friend to Jews. On that the record is clear."

"It is no different in Mystic. What happened here is over. Let it die. Very soon, whatever the disturbance was about, it will be forgotten, and everybody will go on with their lives. This is not the end of the world. It was unfortunate, but it was not a big deal. There are bigger problems for the world to solve. The world is such a crazy place ... just read the papers, you know. Do me a favor. Do this town a favor. Just let it die."

There was a pause. Newman sipped a soft drink. "Mr. Collier, do you think I came her to foul up this town? Hardly. What can I tell you? Sure, President Roosevelt has got bigger problems. France has problems ... Jews have problems, that is for sure. And maybe even tiny Mystic has a few problems, too. But everybody will have bigger problems if people pretend that awful ways of acting are acceptable, or patriotic, or even the right thing to do. What I have always loved about America is a simple ideal; sometimes people have called it the separation of church and state. Other people have expressed it as saying that the laws of our land are blind except for truth. But I like to think of the old revolutionary slogan of 'Don't tread on me' ... you know, the image of the snake all cut up into sections of the country or with one name of a colony from the snake's head right down to its tail. That snake is what we are about. We're a nation that is remarkably alike especially when it comes to injustice. Americans share a deep disdain for being collectively annoyed. Am I explaining this in a way that you can understand?"

And before there was an answer, Newman made time for another single sentence. "Mostly, I came here to see if anybody just wanted to talk. No confrontation."

Michael was a bit exasperated, but he swallowed hard two or three times while containing a quiet rage at this philosophical exercise. "That's good, because there is no need for confrontation around here. People get along, go along, get by. There is nothing to talk about, and there is nothing that

115

needs to be said. You know what I mean? Let this thing die. Forget it. We both know that a lot of things come up short in life ... so what?

Mr. Newman, justice and your philosophy, too, are a crock anyway. Even those who believe that 'good government roots out evil' - even they don't want a town that's empty of prejudice. They want their status, and they want the Jews who live here to recognize them as enlightened. They don't want this place to get beyond their hold. They're more worried that the Irish and the Italians are going to take over. They don't give two whatevers for what the Jews think. Let it go. The Jews will do fine without you or anybody else screaming for justice ... or talk."

Michael was a practical man, or that is what Newman could only surmise. But he was cut from an ancient piece of cloth, the kind of personality and value system that was full of "savvy" to the extent that "savvy" itself was a stereotype. But he was right to think that drawing attention to a problem was never an end in itself, that it was shortsighted and an invitation to shortening the fuse of a problem. A blow-up would occur, but never where it was expected.

What bothered Newman was that Michael lacked a certain sympathy, maybe even something more than sympathy. Questions bother some people, and Newman suspected that Michael was that kind of person. But there was something else about Michael, maybe self- interest that could be nothing but transparent.

As though all conditions in life had built-in carrying charges, even outrage had a price. Was it that Michael was simply adamant about doing business, so adamant that he actually tolerated such victimization? Newman wondered.

Michael believed that social outrage would threaten the people's ability to survive. Newman had a different understanding of the Mystic riot. The episode was more than a struggle between poor Irish and poor Jews. Fear had been used to intimidate people. Perhaps he would not admit it,

116

but Michael was intimidated, too. Michael merely masked his intimidation by adopting an alleged wisdom. Michael feared that examining the problem would only serve to continue the troubles. That was the savvy approach, but fear would be victorious. Newman had no intention of arguing the point, but he believed that the point would inevitably have to be argued.

Michael had forgotten his food. Apparently his energy had seized hold of him to the extent that he could not surrender his argument. "This group you represent is just going to cause trouble and get people excited. This thing will die down, and everybody will forget it. This is America, right? Stop trying to make this something it isn't."

"Sometimes people need to make some waves. People need to take notice when somebody gets cracked in the head. That's all. A message has to be sent out that fear doesn't work. That is a message worth sending." Newman looked directly at Michael. "There's no problem in wanting to know whether the law is being obeyed, is there? No big deal about that."

"Maybe to you it's no big deal, but around here any type of discussion makes people nervous. Why not go on over to Boston or some place that really needs your help. We don't need you. Look, a lot of people think like I do. They plan to stick around, make a living, make more than a living. They plan on doing pretty well. I own a piece of this town - houses and some other buildings. I own property in Boston, too. Publicity screws things up. What do you want out of this place anyway? Those kids who beat up the Suffolk Square crowd, they don't speak for this town. Don't make a crusade out of this thing, because that won't help the Jews here one bit. Stop trying to draw some great moral principle out of this at our expense."

"I don't think I'm trying to make you do anything. Those people who beat up those folks are delinquents. Plain and simple. I heard some accounts of the sentencing. The four boys who were fined were not repentant, and their attorney said as much. All the more reason to send them a message. Those kids are not criminals, but they might turn into criminals if it's easy enough to shut people up. You read the newspapers? Jews are on the run, trying to get out of Hitler's way. But that might not be so easy. Whose way are we getting out of in America? Society needs to speak up. All people, not just Jews, need to draw a line that says that lynchers, Jew haters, anybody who preaches hate is not going to get the applause of society. Society's indifference to injustice is a killer for little towns or big cities or even for whole countries."

Michael's face was strained. Beckah ate her noodle pudding and sipped a soft drink. Her eyes rested on Newman. She said nothing, but she took in every word as though the discussion was a translation of ultimate purposes and not simply words.

"Michael, if I may call you that," Newman spoke in a less strained tone, "I'm not here to cause anybody any trouble. I represent an old and dedicated group that is concerned solely with making certain that people have the opportunity to carry on their lives. The organization thought that this town needed a helping hand. There is a whole history of showing Jews a way when everything else seems to fail. That's our job." Newman paused, aware of a slight stutter that had often caused him to wonder if he was right for this job. "In fact," he finally released his words, "we can do precious little for the people here. Outside of supporting their willingness to meet their problems, we can do little. We point the way; the people have to take it from there."

Michael maintained a somewhat exasperated expression that his voice did not seek to disguise. "Look, we have no real problems. Some kids beat up some old people. It happens. It's a crime. So what? Is that an assault on civilization? We aren't going to change that kind of treatment here or anywhere else. Does it mean that society is collapsing?"

Newman turned toward Beckah. "What would you say if your town could not guarantee public safety to Blacks, Catholics, Jews, gypsies, butterfly enthusiasts, or a travelling baseball team? Wouldn't you wonder what this country was all about?" Newman went on, "Send the signal out that society is watching. Simple stuff. Society needs to keep watch. Shame on us if we're afraid to send that message."

"Newman," Michael interrupted, "maybe you're not interested in making a buck and making a life here in this town, but I and a lot of others are. There is money to be made even in a depression and even in a little town. Real estate is almost being given away. All kinds of people are moving in around here, not just Jews. There is always opportunities and that happens to be what I and this whole country are about. Maybe you're not, but please allow others to live. Time heals all kinds of problems. That's the beautiful thing about this place. That's what's great about America. Time calls the shots. You don't have to make some federal case every time a Jew has a problem. So, Newman, forget the moralizing and leave well enough alone. Thanks for visiting and all that. Forgive me for repeating myself, but we don't need you." Michael got up from his chair. "I'll see you later, Rebecca."

She had said little, but her eyes told another story. She was hurt and perhaps embarrassed. "Jake, my husband has strong views, but he is not an insensitive man. He is concerned about events, but he is concerned about his family, too. Understand?" Newman wanted to help her defend her husband, but he couldn't.

She quickly left the restaurant. Newman remained seated. An older gentleman dressed in an apron and wearing a bow tie wheeled a cart by the table and began to load the empty dishes onto it. The rattling of the dishes and a whirling noise from the kitchen drowned out the silence that existed for at least a few moments.

****

119

Much of Jake's days were spent in a similar way. There were a variety of meetings with all kinds of groups in the community. Some days were devoted to women's gatherings in people's apartments. Many of the streets that converged on Suffolk Square were crammed with row houses, triple-decker structures that had not changed from when Newman was a child. They were more run down, their exteriors showed all the signs of erosion that structures and their inhabitants experience in the space of a very short period of time.

But there was always a great cordiality that Newman was shown. Tea and little pastries or cookies were always offered. Sometimes an older gentleman or two would attend, but mostly Newman found himself in the company of five or six middle-aged women from the neighborhood who wanted to know how to organize the community and go beyond a mere understanding the assault. The violence of that evening made people aware that politics in the community required a vigilance that was without end.

As a result of these meetings, at least two individuals were planning to run for town aldermen positions. Also, a committee for public safety was being established. An effort was underway to create both a YHMA and YHWA, Hebrew men's and women's groups, that would bring people together. Space was rented for young people to go and play pool, or read, or simply find some breathing space beyond their normally tiny, three-decker apartments that surrounded the Square.

Newman attended all these meetings and met the planners and participants, and he listened. Organizing this community had a life of its own. Many people in businesses and professions came forth with suggestions and ideas.

"Mr. Newman, you understand that a rabbi works weekends." Rabbi Kolsky was a frequent participant at the meetings, and Newman enjoyed Rabbi Kolsky's frankness. "An underpaid servant of the people ... but I serve because it is what I do. My wife tells me that her father preferred that she marry a cheese merchant from Kiev. He wanted her to be rich in cheese; he was indifferent to religion. But her mother was against such a match, and her mother ruled the household. So I married a woman who has given me four children, three daughters and a son. And my wife does not hesitate to let me know how better off she would be today had she listened to her father." The Rabbi told his story, and Newman enjoyed every word of it.

"I, of course, use this story, too. I tell my children that the moral of the story is to pay attention to what their father tells them," the Rabbi joked.

"And my wife also uses the story. `Do you see what I mean,' she says to our children. 'One needs to be made of iron to marry a rabbi.'"

In a short amount of time Newman had exchanged hellos and thoughts with many people, and he believed that he had gotten to know much of the flavor of Jewish life in the town.

"You know, Mr. Newman, many people say this is a Yankee town. Others say that this is an Irish town. The Italians call this an Italian town. The Swedes say this town would be nothing without them. Only the blacks and the Jews appear disinterested in claiming the town as their own. They only want the town to change from whatever it is and whoever runs it." Izzy Goldstein was a grocer who loved his own stories, and Newman came to love his stories, too.

"Of course, President Roosevelt says stop bragging and start caring. Ah, there is a mensch!"

****

Spring 1927 ...

Newman had had so many conversations with Mr. Simon that they had become a part of his routine. Simon had an enormous head of gray hair that always seemed to be in need of a good combing. His soft, blue eyes were alert and sensitive to conversation, and Newman sensed that he loved playing with words. His mind was in motion with the first good morning of the day. Just as constant as his good humor were his bow ties. Simon's bow ties fit the hour, the meal being served, and the general routine of the ship's command. Newman joked that merely looking at Simon got him caught in his shipboard duties.

Mr. and Mrs. Simon made frequent trips from New York to Cyprus. On every tour that took Newman to that island, Jake sought out the old man and learned his history. Born in Russia but brought up in Chicago, Mr. Simon retired from the metal spinning business and settled in a suburb of Chicago. The business was now in the hands of their two sons, Arthur and George. "I am a professor emeritus of the business," he joked. "But I have no classes to teach and no students to advise ... maybe I have no job, after all."

"Even when I did have a job I regretted how I had short-changed my education. So many of my days were filled with the pressures and details of operating a business. Each payroll was a monumental challenge - a mountain that required climbing and dexterity or else there was that plunge into the abyss, business failure! So we made some money, then lost it, and made some more ... and the years went by. After a while, I enjoyed the rat race, but there were other things I thought I might enjoy." There was a slight tilt to Mr. Simon's head whenever we had such a discourse. And Newman genuinely liked the gentleman's conversation.

"My passion was reading and, despite the difficulties of my workday, I prided myself on working at different subjects. History was my favorite."

Newman interrupted, "I've always loved history, too. Especially about America or the sea ... anything about the American Revolution. That is my passion."

"Really?" the old man questioned. "That is interesting. Revolutions are fascinating, but the ancient world has always held a special place in my mind. Greece and Rome and the Middle East. Yes, the Middle East has been so full of turbulence, and it remains very much that way today."

Interested in the world about them, Mr. and Mrs. Simon became frequent travellers on the cargo ships of the Merchant Marine fleet. They found the sparse accommodations ample and enjoyed the plentiful food. Mr. Simon satisfied himself with dairy products and vegetables; Mrs. Simon enjoyed any dish that was simple but hearty. Newman went out of his way to see that both of them had plenty of what they liked.

"I am puzzled," the old man once admitted, "as to how the son of a devout Jew found work as a seaman. You do not find such a question too personal, I hope?"

"No. It isn't often anyone asks, though I do ask myself sometimes. At least a ways back I did." Newman enjoyed the old man's questions. He found them insightful. "Mr. Simon, I guess I just enjoy space. I think the sea is something everybody needs sometime in his life. I always liked the combination of open sky and expanses of ocean more than any piece of land I ever put into dock. Does that sound excessively romantic, Mr. Simon?"

"Hardly, Mr. Newman. You have often impressed me as a sensitive fellow. Yet, the world of the son of a traditional Jew and your present world were and are poles apart. To become as you are showed a self-determination that is extraordinary. I wish that I had been as determined as you, my friend. My life was more traditional, one that your father would have favored. That's my guess. But the world cries out for change and for adventure, and it is our duty to listen and respond. At least you seem to have done so."

Newman followed the old man's words and his expressions. There was a wistfulness in his eyes. "It sounds as though you have found some time for change or truth for yourself, Mr. Simon," Newman remarked quite diplomatically.

But Simon replied seriously, "Quite right, Mr. Newman. You are indeed perceptive. The ocean and the sky and my trips on your ship have restored me to life." Now Simon laughed. "Good evening. Thank you, Mr. Newman. I hope our little talks are as enjoyable for you as I find them."

All of this, of course, led to Newman getting his arm gashed and then recuperating in Tiberias. Newman shook his head, thinking about the way time and people pass before one's life. Much like a montage of photographs before his eyes, Newman's mind whirled through those people who had made his merchant marine life ever so complicated. "A fellow goes off to sea to duck out from all his ties only to be caught up in ... commitment," so Newman surmised. Then Simon died, and Mrs. Simon carried on her husband's cause. "If ever there was a revolutionary, it was Mrs. Simon." Newman smiled to himself.

And he wanted to think of Christine McFarland. He could see her scurrying around that hospital ward in her sparkling white uniform, giving orders in an incredibly thick Scottish accent. She had the tiniest, most delicate mouth and a chin that was its match, surrounded by fine blonde hair that hung almost to her shoulders and sort of tossed up near her forehead where the nurses's cap crowned her head. Did Nurse McFarland ever make it out beyond the hospital doors, he wondered to himself? Her skin seemed so fair with only the slightest blush of pink. "She's like a desert flower," Newman liked to say.

"Nurse, do you think that a suffering seaman could get some tea this morning ... maybe with a roll and some jam," he quipped.

"I hear the voice of America calling, do I? No difficulty whatsoever. As long as you can wait for these other fellows to get their medicines, I believe that a call for tea and jam can be respected. You would have these sickly men get their medicines first, would you not, Mr. Newman?"

"Of course, Nurse McFarland. Do you think that we in

America are a species of aborigines? We are sensitive people, we Americans, and we always make way for women, children, the sick, and the aged. But we still like to eat and that includes a daily breakfast. At least a breakfast that precedes our lunch."

"I am sure that all Americans understand the difference between breakfast and lunch, and we in Scotland have no interest in confusing the American people, at least not needlessly confusing them."

"But you do understand the difficulty of having only so many hands, never mind that other individuals might happen to be waiting a great deal longer than you, of course. But this must be all quite incidental to you."

And the banter and the tiny pinches of conversation made the first few weeks of Newman's convalescence fly by. But it was when Newman and his nurse began to walk about the marketplace of the village of Tiberias and to all the nearby ruins that other things occurred.

"What was it about?" Newman wondered. "Was it two lonely people enduring the passage of time?" She was performing service for the Scottish Presbytarian Church, very much as a missionary, and her two years were almost at an end. There was a young man in her life. He was a law student who had finished a military tour in the British army and was about to embark on a legal career. Christine would, doubtless, marry that fellow, although Newman was never exactly certain if that had occurred.

She was an evangelical Protestant providing service to the world ("living the gospel" as she called it), and he was an American seaman, a non-practicing Jew indifferent to religion but mixed up with a retired businessman-turned Zionist revolutionary. Simple enough.

"Was it any wonder that the two of us found peace in each other's company and in each other's sense of life?" Tiberias was a sleepy, mostly Arab and Christian town. While the Sea of Galilee gently rolled and splashed upon its shores, tropical plants, flowers and tall, leafy Mediterranean trees made the passage of time slow and wonderfully unimportant.

Chapter Eight

You Are All Cousins

Newman sometimes would reflect on his life as a seaman. The bonds that grew between members of the crew were like those of an athletic team which builds from the practice fields to the stadium and then to the final moments before its contest. Newman was appreciative of such camaraderie.

Henry McNulty was a favorite mate of Newman's. A Nova Scotian, he had grown up with the sea. His stubby beard and wind-burned face marked him as an outdoors man. McNulty was not a sentimentalist. "The ocean is no man's friend," he liked to say. "When you start looking to the sea for companionship, you better get your ass out of the water. You're a gonna."

But McNulty loved ships. He understood the balance that a load of cargo played in keeping a ship on a steady course through the choppiest of seas. "All I want is a steady ship and some Ballentine brew," he loved to repeat. His red-veined face and swollen nose bore testimony to his words.

Sometimes Jim Spinney, his old friend from Mystic, would sail with Newman. Newman, in fact, had helped Spinney's mother accept her son's decision to join the merchant seamen. Mrs. Spinney delighted in Newman's good humor and, what she called, his healthy attitude about the world. She was impressed by his abandon of the measured life. She had been born in the Irish ward of the city, where males beyond high-school age made their way to labor in the tanneries or the rubber factories or drifted away from the town.

"Son," she said to Spinney, "if the choice is between you as a drifter or a factory slave, then I'd have you be a drifter. Make the life you want. I know what the factory can do to people. You don't need this town. You never did."

Spinney's father was a New England man whose lineage meant less to him than his numerous children. Newman recalled trekking with Spinney to a cemetery on the New Hampshire border one hot day. The "ancestral" cemetery was a series of gravestones of farmers and working hands so numerous as to have a lake, a street, and the cemetery itself named after them.

Spinney had not been impressed with his family's importance to the community. He shared Newman's pessimism about worldly conventions. At odds with his neighbors and family, Spinney, like a frustrated American pioneer, needed trees and fields to give him a feeling of independence. His contempt for authority was one of the qualities that Newman most admired.

And then there was another seaman's voice.

"I see that one of your cousins got himself blown up." There was a sharpness to John Henderson's voice that matched the roughness of his words. Newman looked up. "Your pal, Simon," Henderson continued impatiently. "You know, the old guy that sailed with us. He got himself smashed up by a British frigate outside of Haifa. Paper says he was a gun-runner. Shot trying to escape. That's what those damn boxes of his contained. Guns. He was supplying guns to some Jews in Palestine."

"My cousin?" he thought and then understood. To Henderson all Jews were cousins, part of a tribe. Funny, the old man once said to him, "Mr. Newman, some people say that we Jews are a tribe. But I have always felt that what makes a tribe is a common passion, the common perception of either a friend or foe. That perception occurs to many people across all kinds of geography, even the geography of birth."

"I don't have a problem with that, Mr. Simon, but I have heard lots of slurs about tribes. Irish tribes, Italian tribes, Black tribes ... doesn't it all come down to doing surgery on people? Trying to neatly tie up a group for the usual purpose of sticking something up their collective asses?" Newman's remarks were delivered coolly and calmly, suggesting that this was not the first time he had dealt with the variations on the notion of "tribe".

"Well, we shall see, Mr. Newman. I have a special favor to ask of you. As you know Palestine is full of different people who share a singular obsession: distrust. Some people quite close to me, I will call them part of a tribe, need some assistance, and I immediately thought of you. Have you ever played pin the tail on the donkey?"

"Haven't we all?" Newman answered, but he prepared himself for a reply possibly at the opposite end of the question.

"Do not look so anxious, Mr. Newman. My question is a simple one. When playing pin the tail on the donkey, it is common to fix a pin on almost any part of the donkey's anatomy. Isn't that one of the charms of the game? What is more delightful than to see the nose of the beast become the resting place for their tail ... or even the great body of the beast suddenly decorated with a hairy and bushy tail? So it is in Mideast politics. One never knows where the tail will be placed.

In fact, the placement of the tail reveals the intentions of the players. Take the British. They mean well, but they have yet to admit that self-interest is the only basis for their control in the world. As soon as anyone asks the British to be fair or equitable on a matter that they believe to be at some distance from their pocketbooks, they certainly buckle under the pressure. That is why both the Arabs and the Jews so dislike the British authority in Palestine. Only the Arabs are assured that the British will cooperate because Arabs hold the keys to all kinds of natural resource explorations that take place continually in this rich but divisive land. As for the Jews, they possess only urgency, only desperation. This is where you can help ... on placing the donkey's tail."

"My help?" Newman questioned.

"Yes."

"The British had been watching him for a while," Henderson went on. "Heh, they were probably watching you too, Newman. The way you guys were always yapping." Henderson wanted Newman to know the extent of his information. "A British ship fired on his boat about two miles off of Haifa. The ship was all but blown apart, but they found his body."

"And his wife?"

"No mention of her. But if she's involved, she'd better watch out. The British mean business, especially with Jews in Palestine. Makes the Arabs nervous." Chuckling, Henderson left. Newman went inside in search of a newspaper.

The article confirmed Henderson's words. Moreover, Newman knew the background which the report had omi ted. Clandestine military units were a part of the Palestine landscape. Officers aboard the merchant marine ships that carried goods to Jaffa and Haifa had been warned to avoid getting duped. Newman recalled a Captain Kearney's words, "Carrying guns, ammunition, or even Red Cross material angers the British, who have controlled Palestine since the end of World War I. They get so angry they may hang the guilty or set up a firing squad. Such events are not part of our work schedule." Captain Kearney possessed a sense of humor. He had followed his warning with a graphic description of doing time in a British jail. "The food stinks, and physical abuse is a tradition. Avoid long stays with British soldiers."

****

Newman remembered receiving only two messages aboard the vessel. One concerned the death of his father. A radio message, it had been transmitted as a courtesy while Newman was headed to Havana. "Your father, David Newman, passed away on May 16, 1915. Funeral is May 17, 1915. Sincere sympathy, Captain Murray." It had reached him on May 29th. His other communication had been a request from Jim Spinney, in need of a $100 bond posted to a Norfolk, Virginia, jail. It was unusual, then, for Newman, whose ship was docked in Haifa, to receive a telegram from Gerda Simon. "Mr. Newman, the death of my husband forces me to ask a favor," it read. "Please contact me at 159 Abendstrasse at your earliest convenience. G. Simon."

Newman loved the hills of Haifa and the Middle- Eastern and European flavor of its stores and parks. Its neatly laid out streets made Haifa unlike any of the cities in Palestine that he was familiar with.

In an apartment building four stories tall with a balcony overlooking the Mediterranean, Newman found Mrs. Simon. Entering, he noticed the heavy, dark furniture and the variety of different shaped mirrors displayed on nearly all the walls. Mrs. Simon was a small woman whose eyes and skin revealed a time-worn look - puffy eyes and tired, inelastic skin. Her hair was mostly gray with a glimmer of black. She remained seated in a large, upholstered chair as Newman entered the room. She wore a flowered, blue dress. There was animation in her face as she greeted Newman.

"Your coming here means a great deal to me, Mr. Newman," she began. "It confirms my husband's judgment that you are a caring young man. 'A sympathetic young man,' that is what Julius would say." Mrs. Simon motioned him to an armchair beside the chair in which she was seated; nearby was a glass coffee table. "Would you like some ice tea?" she offered, tilting her head just as her husband had done when he spoke.

"Yes, that would be great," Newman answered.

In seconds, a tall glass was poured from a blue glass pitcher. Mrs. Simon did not waste a step.

"You see, Mr. Newman, my husband's death remains more than my own loss. His work here in Palestine was to assure desperate people that they had a refuge. Those same people need me now as they needed him before. Would you like a bit more?" Mrs. Simon began to pour when Newman nodded. "These people need you, too, Mr. Newman. You may be able to help us."

"Mrs. Simon," Newman interrupted, "the newspaper said that your husband was killed running guns into Palestine. He was named as part of an anti-British underground, part of a violent Zionist movement. Newman bluntly stated what he had read. He was on guard. The lady facing him might look like a lovely grandmother, but Newman remembered that her husband had looked equally harmless.

Mrs. Simon took his remarks easily. "Certainly, Mr. Newman, both he and I have been committed to Jewish Palestine. Violent? We are not violent. But there is violence out there, in our country. That we know, and Julius' death is part of that violence. One does not need to be a Jew to understand all that; one simply needs to be young, or old, or a thinking person! My husband met a violent end because individuals working on behalf of the British government in Palestine refused to recognize the Zionist dream. But despite their hard-heartedness and all that such a disposition robs from our lives, we will persevere, Mr. Newman. Rest assured of that." She spoke forcibly but without emphasis or even solemnity.

"Mr. Newman, we know that American Merchant Marines travel to the ports of Palestine and to cities throughout the Mediterranean. That is why my husband and I frequented ships such as the one we met you on. British port inspectors tolerate American ships and American crews. It is understood that the Merchant Marines are in the business of commerce - legal, international commerce. What is less well-known is the relative ease that oversees such trade. This is not a criticism, just a statement of fact."

Leaning against a bureau was a box four feet long and a foot in width. Mrs. Simon pointed to it. "You carried hundreds of boxes like this for my husband," she said as she unfolded the top of the box and began to remove some of its contents. "Here, for example, is a window shade." She lowered a tube-like band of gray paper to the bottom of her feet holding the top of the shade to her head. "Six shades occupy

134

each box." As she unrolled the shades, she revealed a gun barrel that could be joined to a variety of mechanisms that were hidden in the panels of the box. She continued, "Everything is manufactured in France and shipped by the shade company. A variety of parts can be brought in at one time or over several shipments to our friends." Casually, Mrs. Simon removed two panels from the walls of the box; each wall contained rows of bullet shells.

It seemed to Newman that the arsenal displayed in front of him was totally incongruous to the dignified woman seated next to him. There was, however, a determination about Mrs. Simon that could not be mistaken. She was the epitome of business. As she easily explained what she wanted from Newman, her direct manner and sense of purpose became evident.

"You want me to help you smuggle this package beyond the British customs inspectors? Those officers aren't fools."

"Of course not, Mr. Newman, but they trust you. Frequently, I saw them joking with you when they boarded your ship. Maybe it will take theatrics or a bribe, but that's what I need to ask of you. I need your help. Maybe we could unload these materials a day earlier or keep it on board, out of the way, until the time is right. We are flexible, but we need your help. Again she poured the tea as Newman agreed to have a bit more. She was flexible; that she was.

****

When Newman entered his hotel, Mr. Ginsburg, looking dapper in a light-blue bow tie, was at the front desk.

"We must be getting a cool east wind, Mr. Ginsburg." Newman joked, "I don't think I've ever seen you wearing a tie before."

"Do you like it? My wife makes them, so naturally I wear them. But you are right, Mr. Newman, the weather is wonderful. The radio says that it will be cool for about three days. Cold Canadian air. Here they call it a "Canadian Express". In the summer it is wonderful, but in the winter it means a chilling frost that wraps the land in a cold box. Isn't the weather one of life's delights?"

"Mr. Ginsburg, once again, you have said it all," Newman laughed as he turned to go to his room.

"But, Mr. Newman, wait! I have a message for you. Attorney Joruchoff was here looking for you. He asked that you meet him at the Evening News office at six. He has arranged a meeting that he'd like you to attend."

Newman glanced at his watch. It was just past noon. "Thanks for the message." He waved a goodbye and started to climb the stairs up to his room.

Entering the bedroom, he noticed that there was a cool breeze that lifted the white curtains deep into the room. He immediately got to work. For the better part of the afternoon, he banged the keys of his typewriter. Finished, he tucked the typewritten pages into an envelope and addressed it to his New York office. He wanted to rest at that point, but he was too restless. He had too much energy, so he resumed typing.

This time the subject was Mystic and the way ethnic turmoil assaults the sensibilities of reasonable people. He wrote as an intermediary exposing bigotry and explaining to victim and victimizer that fear and injustice are kindred emotions. What Newman typed out was a confession of his faith. In his confession, Newman sought to understand all who trespass and all who suffer. He reflected how he, too, was victim and victimizer. He had spoken evil, had performed acts of violence, had criss-crossed all the boundaries that no person can justify. And what of punishment, he wondered. Punishment? The only punishment is to attest to one's failing: to stand before those you have wronged and to admit wrong. And then there is the need to help those who have been wronged, to have the strength to stand before those who have suffered and to try to make some redress. That is bearing witness. To help the transgressors look at their victims and to admire them - that, too, is bearing witness.

A faint knock at his door interrupted the click of the striking keys. Opening the door, Newman faced Beckah. He once again noticed the youthful fullness to her face despite the sunglassses and the pink, summer dress. What was it about this woman that made him ever so curious about her, Newman thought. And his mind thought once again of the fairy tale character Snow White. That was it. Her white skin that was fair and extraordinarily soft and beautiful; her lips that were full and red; her hair, tied up and pushed to the back - everything about her reminded him of Snow White.

"Thanks for coming to the party. I was glad to see you, but I am sorry we didn't have a chance to talk." She took her sunglasses off, and Newman nodded to her and himself. Yes, her eyes were blue. "May I come in?"

"Of course. Sorry, I have little to offer you, I'm afraid." With her hands she gestured not to worry.

Newman continued. "You were more than busy and there were many guests for you to welcome. I was happy to meet your daughter. Her name is Sarah?" Newman asked.

"Right, Sarah is wonderful. She's clever and full of warmth, and she has been an incredible part of my life ... I can still remember her as a five year old."

Newman's face exhibited some puzzlement.

"Sarah is Michael's daughter from his first marriage. She was five when Michael and I got married."

"She has a certain smile and a glow that are quite appealing. She made me think of you when I saw her."

"Thank you," Beckah said. "Sarah is my child and always has been. She and Allen are lovely people. I'm happy for them, and I'm worried for them, too. The world is so crazy - the war in Europe, this depression, just so many uncertainties."

She sat on a chair to the right of the table where Newman

had been working. Her eyes encouraged Newman to sit. "I wanted to speak with you. Something bothered me about the other night, when we were speaking about Jenny. I'm not sure I said what I felt."

"Jenny was not some crazy person. She was a wonderful person. More than anybody, you've got to know that." Beckah was ill-at-ease; she struggled trying to find a comfortable position in the straight-backed chair. After a while, she settled into a spot that gave her body and her mind the ease to continue and to probe what she deeply felt.

"Jenny was too good; she was almost like a child. She was lost in a kind of goodness. Oh, she was no fool. She saw people for what they were, sadly. Take the college. The college! The college was a house of cards, and those were her words. Isn't that the case? A house of cards with professors more groping than the students. The administrators were cut from yet another piece of cloth: anxious, nervous about admitting too many Jews or an all too infrequent Black. Nervous about the number of Jews on the faculty ... or the "right kind" of woman that they'd hire maybe every ten years. The college was simply a halfway house, never sure who were its clients or what was its mission. And Jenny saw that. Maybe she saw it a bit late in her life, only because she spent so many years of her life there.

And when she spoke about the college, she would mention you. 'Jake,' she'd say, 'was from the lower depths of the social heap and he knew it. He was a bright guy who didn't want to be one of the poor, deserving Jews that the admissions people had to admit.'

That honesty was part of Jenny's charm, too. Her family paid for her education, and she wasn't self- conscious about coming from a working-class background. Working in a college library was different than having to deal with people in a factory or even in a bank. There was a certain isolation to her life, and Jenny nurtured that part of her until, I think, she came to almost despise herself."

138

"She called herself the 'Jewish librarian ... the college's Jewish librarian'. She sometimes laughed about it, but at other times it bothered her. She did love to read and to think of herself as a literary sort, and she was. But there was also a feeling of being trapped that made her angry and frustrated. Do you know that she discovered she was only the second Jewish person to work in the library, that is as a full-time employee?"

Newman accepted the pause in Beckah's voice and asked, "And there was no place to go and no reason to try someplace else?"

"I think that's about right. She'd made a kind of peace with her life, and I don't really know all the other pieces it may have contained. Who can say? She loved to work with children. She'd read Bible stories to them and try to make them comfortable understanding what she felt was a special religious identity ... an identity as a people. Jenny wanted them to understand that they were an ancient people and the world was God's gift to them. She'd have them do drawings, and sing songs, and celebrate holidays in a fun way and with delight. The parents loved the way she worked with the kids."

"How did she put it? 'Your life is part of a larger life, like a ball of twine, so let's think about one another as though we are parts of the same piece of string. Understanding the world and the Jewish laws is a part of that ball of twine.' She'd talk about this to the parents, too. And they nodded and said sure, sure, sure."

"You're losing me. What is it you are telling me?" Newman asked.

"They mocked her. They thought she was daffy. Ball of string, your ass, if you know what I mean. They were interested in their homes, their automobiles, their businesses, and keeping ahead of the depression ... the usual private lives mindset, despite the way things were changing. To Jenny, the beginning of the war in Europe and the kind of prejudice that was popping out of every crack in America, never mind in Europe, made her crazy. The Father Coughlins and the Gerald Smiths and the little bands of local fascists changed her, frightened her to a kind of desperation."

"She didn't know what to make of things; she didn't know how to go on with a librarian's life."

Beckah's voice trembled. "People looked at her as though she were crazy, over-reacting, overly sensitive - that sort of thing. The world wasn't crazy, she was. Do you know what I'm trying to tell you?"

"I think so. It sounds like she was quite alone and afraid, but no one cared."

"Yes. Very much like that. There was no one, no one to help her or help what was going on. There was just a great darkness about America and Europe, and it all hit her."

Beckah reached into her purse; Newman paid little attention as she did so. He was caught up in her words and how her words made him think about his similar feelings. Beckah took a large, manilla envelope from her bag; it was folded in two and was kept in place by an enormous red elastic band.

"These are some of Jenny's things ... her writings over the last two years. She had given them to me; I thought she just wanted me to read them, but she meant more than that. She gave them to me the way one gives away things before one moves or dies. I didn't realize that till she died. But that is why I have these things. I've gone through them at least a dozen times ... poems, a diary, little remembrances, even some songs - songs for children and other songs, too. I never realized how clever and insightful she was ... how unusual."

Beckah handed the folded envelope to Newman. "Jake, I want you to read these things. They need to be read. They are extraordinary, and I don't know who else to give them to."

Newman took the poems. "I'm going to give them back to you, but I want to see them. There has got to be a place for things like this, but first I want to read them. Even as a kid she wrote poems. So did I. I guess she never stopped. Thanks for letting me see them. Really, you cared about her."

"I did. I did care."

"She was lucky." And Newman thought about the kind of loneliness that he had known, and he thought about Jenny's loneliness. Somehow, it was odd to him that it was Beckah who had brought all of this back to him. From the first moment he set his eyes upon her, Beckah was the one that made him remember Jenny and even things about himself.

"That ball of string ... there is a great deal to that, don't you think?" Beckah asked.

Newman nodded.

"I do. I think of that, and I think about all that she went through. And I think about this town and even you." As Beckah said this, it was clear that there was a certain courage and even hope that was a part of her words. She looked at Newman and her eyes were bright and quite blue, and there was a great sense of giving that her eyes gave forth.

As though the room tilted and as though all the world was drawn close together, Newman reached for her hand and then both of their hands met. With each of their hands in the clasp of the other, Newman drew her close to him and he kissed her.

"I have never kissed a married woman before," Newman whispered. "But I have never wanted to kiss someone as I have wanted to kiss you."

She smiled and held him close to her, close to her to feel his warmth and even to sense his embrace. "Jake, I don't know how to explain it, but you have brought something to me, to my life, that I did not know existed." And Beckah reached his lips with her own and there was a silence, a long moment of silence just as when one sees a rolling wave, and only sees it but does not hear it rumble or crash. Their embrace was all that competed for that moment. Only the silence of that moment mattered.

Newman's mind was not racing. He was not concerned about his present or his past. He closed his eyes but still could see that something unusual had happened to him. Let it be called whatever it would be. Newman felt at ease, at rest, but also quite grateful.

"I have to go," Beckah said as she rose from her chair. She placed her arm on Newman's shoulder. "I'll see you." She kissed him on his cheek, and then she kissed his lips.

****

Alone with his thoughts and his bundle of Jenny's letters and poems, Newman felt many things. Many feelings coursed through his body; many years tumbled through his mind. But he was not unhappy, even thinking of Jenny's face and her smile - a smile that grew in radiance the way a morning sky grows fully blue and bright. He was perplexed by Jenny's fate, but he did not want that to alter his picture of her face or the kind of glory she brought to the days that they shared. Jenny was secure in his heart and his mind. She fit and belonged in a way that was not to be altered. He was content in his certitude of that.

"And what of Beckah?" aloud he asked himself.

And though he was weary by just about everything that had brought him back to Mystic, he somehow felt that Beckah helped. Beckah helped him be strong and, in her way, assured him that all was on course. That was it, Newman repeated. Beckah makes me feel on course ... that there is a plan, that there is some wisdom in the way the world works despite so many reasons to doubt and even to feel despair.

"Odd. Even though she is married, her strength helps me. She can handle it. She knows this is right." And Newman knew that she was right for him, too. As he tried to explain this to himself, Newman realized that an explanation was not necessary. Instead, he felt an ease and a certainty and

even an eagerness to allow whatever life, whatever present-
ness he could bring to his life, to simply proceed. Did Beckah
look as contentedly upon these last days of August as
Newman did?

****

Somewhere near the end of the collection of papers that
Beckah had left, Newman came across what must have been
portions of Jenny's diary that were not dated. For a good
period of that day Newman had difficulty reading or thinking
about anything else.

From Jenny's diary ...

You have to hear it from me. You have to stop guessing
about my life and, because I want you to know me, I must
tell you. I despise the unexamined life. I despise all the silly
conversations that are nothing more than expressions of
polite manners. Every idea is not a life or death consideration, but spare me the endless prattle that takes the sun-
shine out of the finest Spring day.

Say something. Say something. Say something, anything
that tells me you have noticed my brain, my person, my
humanity. Something that tells me about everything that is
your humanity. Please, say something, not for me, but for
you!

Of course, I want you to read my diary, just as I want my
poems read and my songs sung. Of course I do. Maybe I
thought too much of myself. Perhaps far too much of myself.
So? So what? I've written five poems that have found their
way into print, and I have earned $200 for two and a half
decades of work. I have never heard one of my songs sung,
that is, if you do not consider the sounds they make in my
brain. Have I thought too much of myself? Have I been too
harsh on those who have no interest in poems or songs?

143

Have I been unkind to those who have minimized what a poem or a song can bring to a morning or nighttime? Tell me. Please tell me if I have been unkind.

The children know. The children care about things that matter - sounds, caring eyes, a game. They notice the trees, whether they are full of greenness or without a leaf. The children know. They are of the world. Bravely, they try to be themselves and can be even unafraid to say they are sorry. They, of course, will not be children forever. Nor could I.

Maybe I missed my life. Maybe it escaped me or fooled me. Maybe I did think it belonged one place, then another place, but each place was a mistake. I did not know it at the time. I don't know it now. What has passed in front of my eyes has left me convinced that a little is better than none, that words are wonderful, that my name and my person sing, and that New England runs through my heart.

I am sure of these things, and I do not expect to change my mind. Have I been harsh? Has the rain soaked into the ground?

Chapter Nine

Unto the Tribe

The building that housed the town's police department was built on the side of a hill. Its large oak door was simply marked "Police". When Newman entered the anteroom, he noticed an air of officialdom and a quiet that mirrored the weather.

"I wonder if the chief is around?" Newman asked. His voice was so matter of fact that he was surprised.

"And who is asking?" the young officer manning the front desk replied.

"Jake Newman. I'm an investigator for the Organization of American Hebrew Aid." Newman noticed an expression of annoyance on the lieutenant's face. What could be wrong, Newman wondered. Did the name 'American' illicit the officer's frown, or was it the word 'Hebrew', or perhaps the combination of both? Whatever.

"You are an investigator?" the lieutenant asked. "You have some questions ... about what?"

"Just a few. But listen, before I waste any more of your time, I am an old friend of the chief's. He knows me. We go back a ways."

"The name was Newman, right? I'll tell him you're here."

In a moment, the officer returned. "He says to go on in." Though the lieutenant continued to spy him through the corners of his eyes, he led Newman into the chief's office.

Bare of just about everything, a desk and two chairs comprised the total furnishings of the office. A sign over the door announced the occupant, Chief James Spinney. The darkstained and oiled wooden floors creaked at Newman's every step. And the squeaky floors made Newman think of all the old New England buildings that were built to last forever. Comfort, of course, was a stranger to all who either worked or visited these edifices. There were two, tall window frames that almost reached to the ceiling of the room that were well over ten feet high. From the windows only the thick greenery of trees could be seen.

Raising his head, the chief said simply, "That you, Jake?"

146

There were no other words.

With affection, Newman responded, "Hey, Jim, your voice hasn't changed. But you're a lot bigger than I remember ... or does that desk only make you look that way?"

The chief laughed. "Funny, you always were a hot one, Jake. What is it twenty years, and the first thing I hear is how fat I am?"

The signs of mid-life were there. Spinney's gray hair now had the same widow's peak his father had had. The prominent waistline was an admission that Jim's days as an athlete had passed.

"Only kidding you. You look good, Jim. Really."

"I look like hell and you know it." Jim stretched out his hand and laughed a bit harder. "But you're the same. You haven't changed. How do you do it?"

"I look as god-awful as you, Jim. But that's little consolation for either of us. I credit all my attributes, including my good looks, to paying no attention."

"Jake, who cares? We're alive. That's got to count for something." There was a broad smile and a genuine glad-to-see you feeling that Jim exuded and that Newman remembered as typical of his old friend.

"Survival counts for something. I just don't know what. Look at you. You came back. You're the chief of this place?" Newman asked rhetorically, but he did not wait for a response.

Newman's voice was full of irony. "Both of us finally came back. My old man would get a kick out of that."

"It's the way it goes. Suddenly you realize that there is nowhere to go. I had nowhere else to go. It was time to get on with it, Jake. Time to put the merchant marines and all of the travelling and all the stuff of a seaman's life out of my head. I'd had it with the merchant marines, may the Lord look after each and every soul in that navy."

Newman understood. He'd done the same, though he had started life anew with a different address. For a second, he saw himself and his friend in their khaki uniforms. There was an enormous sun in the background; then that enormous sun was shaken by the explosion of a gun that brought Newman out of his reverie.

Spinney continued, "When that problem down in Suffolk Square broke out, I expected there would be some fallout ... I don't know, a demonstration or something. Something that was meant to be symbolic, if you follow me. Something that would send out a message." Jim talked with his hands, and Newman enjoyed the energy and incisiveness of his friend.

"But I didn't expect to see you turn up. Not now, not ever. That was a surprise. Is that what it took to get you back here? Wait a second. Maybe I'm not surprised, but seeing you sure does bring back the memories. I'm the chief. Isn't that a kick in the ass?" There was a cawing sound coming from birds nearby and Spinney remarked, "Listen to those birds. They even think its funny. Remember as kids we'd say that the birds are laughing at us. Remember?"

Newman nodded and he laughed a bit. "Seems like the birds around here always laughed at us," Newman said.

Spinney looked at Newman with a twist of a smile. "We shoot chiefs of police, don't we, Jake?"

That took the smile off of Jake's face. Jim, too, was staring straight ahead. There was a recognition of some memory that took command of both of their minds, a memory that had notched each of them as a tree is scarred by an axe.

"We gave it some thought; we did once." Newman was meeting up with a part of his past. He felt no sentiment or guilt over Spinney's remark. It was true. "We need a drink. What do you think, Jim?" Newman asked. "It's not too early is it?"

"Not for a drink." The chief grabbed his cap, and they both walked past the officer at the desk. "I'm out for a bit," the chief remarked and shut the door behind him.

Together on the street of their boyhood, the two men found they still held a sense of who they were.

"Like the merchant marines, Jake, a drink before noon."

They laughed as the chief opened the door of his Dodge with Mystic Police Chief printed in black letters on the door. The car angled through the meandering streets of the downtown area, full of shops and morning shoppers. Newman recognized buildings in the business district. They rode by the library built by the American architect, Henry Hobson Richardson. Its Romanesque arches and reddish-stone impressed him just as it had many years ago.

"This library really is a fine building," he remarked.

The chief nodded and continued driving toward the west end of town.

****

"You better watch out that your shoes don't get sucked up into the mud," he warned her. "That ground is soft. Walk along the trunk of this tree."

Jenny was not adventurous, but she was athletic. It was easy for her to keep her balance. Newman remembered how her mother had objected to her little girl riding the rafts on the backwaters of the swamp, pants full of mud, shoes covered by the reeds of the swamp.

"The rafts were great, weren't they?" he remembered saying.

"Great," she had agreed. And they both understood that the times they shared were delightful moments of their lives together. Newman had held her arm as she made her way along the birch's bough, and their faces had been but an inch apart. He kissed her; and she quietly tilted her head toward his lips. Their lips met in a kiss that brought them together in a way that neither time nor life could change.

"I love you, Jake."

"I love you, too," Newman whispered.

Jenny was three years younger, a world of difference when you're a teenager. He remembered thinking then that their paths would never again cross. She was a student; he was not. She would be headed for college; he was headed for anywhere the railroad would take him. Jenny's kindness and innocence were qualities he admired. Newman didn't see any qualities in himself that someone might find worth caring about. That Jenny saw anything in him was a mystery, but Newman was too pleased to be in her company, never mind in her arms, to delve into it. The young girl's soul had worked itself into his heart. "If I could feel this way forever," he had thought.

****

"Jake. Jake. You aren't fogging out on me, are you?" Spinney's voice penetrated Newman's reverie.

"No, not me, Jim."

The chief's car had made its way to a hilly dirt road in a part of town that Newman did not recognize. "Where the hell is this?"

"You don't remember this place? This is the place where we used to swim when we were kids."

"Old man Whipple's place?"

"Right. Remember he used to walk that damn German shepherd of his and chase us out of here. Who was it? Was it Eliot or Johnny Meagher swimming in his pond, and he told him to stay right there or he'd set the dog on him?"

"It was Johnny."

"Right. 'You're bluffing!' Johnny had yelled at him. And that mother of a dog raced after him and grabbed him by his ass which was half way up a tree."

They both laughed.

They came to the chief's house, high on a hill in the most western part of town. It was a rambling Victorian with three porches devoid of paint.

"If you think this place needs work," the chief remarked, looking carefully at Newman's face, "you should have seen it when I bought it. An old guy had lived here for about forty years, the last twenty alone after his sister passed away. Then it really was a wreck. But my wife liked the place, and the price was right. I was a patrolman then and money was piss poor, so we bought it and have been fixing it up ever since. It will never get finished the way I want, but Sharon just minds a little. You don't know her. She was a few years younger than us. She lived in Everett. If it hadn't been for Sharon, I'd have been a drunk or a road bum a long time ago."

Once inside, Spinney went to the kitchen to pour out two substantial glasses of whiskey. Newman stayed on the porch. He sat in one of the two wicker chairs and looked about him, admiring a garden of late blooming irises and what looked like a variety of shasta daisies, all neatly coordinated around a bed of different colored stones.

"Thanks," he said as the chief gave him his drink." A side table also made of the same white wicker was covered by a piece of glass cut into the shape of an oval, and Newman placed his glass on the tabletop. "This is peaceful. You know, as a kid I'm not sure I realized how quiet it is around here. It sure is quiet now ... except for the birds and especially the crows. Geez, are there crows, enough crows to keep every farmer in New Hampshire awake at night."

But Newman suddenly stopped talking and noticed the silence that had set in. Then Jake recognized that the silence needed to be explored for what it actually was, a pause before the memories of Palestine took over. It was their common past.

****

February, 1928 ...

Smuggling guns into Palestine was one of the few objectives shared by Arabs and Jews, even if the purposes of the weapons were to obliterate one another. But there were some variations. The Arabs had the advantage of using land routes, and a brisk business of carrying arms was conducted by trucks, rail, and the more picturesque caravan.

For the Jews the sea provided the best route for smuggling munitions and medical supplies, all contraband for everybody except the Jews. In the most obscure parts of ships, laden with apples or other agricultural produce, were stashed the essentials of maintaining a struggle. Later, these essentials would be unloaded to a truck or an automobile for another journey to a cellar or dug out or disguised countryside location.

British responsibility for the people within Palestine was a result of the League of Nation's policy of providing governance for areas that ultimately would become sovereign. This was the formal explanation of a most complex Colonial presence. The British style of governance suggested that aspiring for self- determination was not an end unto itself. A certain earning of one's independence needed to occur. The British established themselves as a ruler that needed to be reassured that independence could work. Arguments that British self-interest worked against home rule were dismissed out of hand or merely viewed as badgering a western power. Experience, the British claimed, validated the need for a Colonial government to be exact and explicit when dealing with a native population. The prerogatives of government bore responsibility to the world, even if the locals needed to be reminded of their place.

In the meantime, Palestine was home to a multitude of struggling forces of religious Jews, Christians, Zionists, and Arabs. Throughout the 1920s and into the 1930s, Jewish philanthropists had purchased land within Palestine so that Jewish people and Jewish ideology could come to the land of their fathers. These men and women of the business world were making a nation before any formal nation existed. Julius and Gerda Simon were such individuals.

Julius Simon understood shipping schedules and how to package materials, having once owned a small business. When he retired, Simon was determined to place his energies and expertise in a struggle dear to his heart. Getting illicit cargoes into ports controlled by British customs officers and the British military was formidable but not without precedent. Simon was a master of the artful concealment of weapons. In addition, he understood how to shepherd these weapons through the most bureaucratic customs systems, relying on the tools of smuggling: favors, bribes, and threats.

"I gave my business some of the best years of my life. I deserve to use my remaining years for a cause that means something," Simon announced to his wife.

"It is a little like burying treasure," Gerda remarked.

"Exactly, my dear. Buried treasure. I don't know where these shipments will wind up, but I do know that our job is to get them to Palestine. Sometimes the best way to get goods by the customs inspectors is to have those inspectors carry the goods out for you." That became the basis of their plans.

To further this plan of his and a number of like- minded individuals, Simon called on Ian Marcus, a British official of marginal importance in British Palestine but who possessed a supervisory position in customs. Marcus' face was moon-shaped, and he had a ruddy complexion. His head was perpetually covered with a sun-hat that may have shaded his bulging eyes but did not protect him from the uncomfortable Palestine heat.

Despite the temperature, however, Marcus found his post enjoyable because he recognized the superiority of working for the British government outside of Britain as opposed to working for the same government at home. Marcus' wife was South American. Neither Simon nor anyone else knew anything about their home life. Marcus had served throughout the British empire in one civil servant capacity after another. For a time he had worked in India. A few years before the outbreak of the Great War, he had been part of the British

153

legation in the Middle East.

Though he enjoyed diplomatic society, Marcus disliked the administrative duties of governing and making decisions which might eventually lead to his downfall as they had done to many a civil servant before him. Marcus did not like to offend. Marcus had one talent. At government receptions, the tall, slender British official could drink enormous quantities of anything as long as it didn't cost him anything.

For the four months that Newman worked with Mrs. Simon, most of his time was spent guiding dories or motorized craft from a ship to a deserted beach on the Palestine coast. As soon as the boxes of materials arrived, they were loaded into the trucks hidden nearby. Young girls drove the trucks. Once the shipments were delivered, Newman never saw the materials or the loaders again.

"What is your name?" Newman had asked a dark-haired girl.

"Shana. My name is Shana." She smiled and Newman saw how lovely she was. In America, this girl might have had a sheltered, secure life. Here she was driving a truck and risking her life for a cause most people had no idea even existed. This impressed Newman because girls and boys like Shana made the "revolution" so powerful and convincing, yet so vulnerable.

"I know why they call you Shana," Newman had told her.

She smiled, acknowledging the unspoken compliment.

"Shana, get your truck and yourself out of here as fast as you can. Stay well." Newman admired this lovely young woman joined in the cause for which he was working

"You and your friend, Mr. Spinney, have helped us a great deal, Mr. Newman," Mrs. Simon offered at the conclusion of a late transfer of goods.

"Well, this is about the end of the line for us. Our ship will be picking us up in three or four days. We did what we could." Newman looked at Mrs. Simon with admiration but with some exhaustion, too.

Spinney had pulled the wooden dory onto the beach, but only his shadow could be seen because the sky was so dark. Spinney waved letting Newman know that the job was done.

"Your friend and you have helped us," Mrs. Simon resumed, "and we are thankful. My husband felt that you were the perfect person for such a task, a good person who hated injustice. My husband understood people."

"Your people need a lot more than me or Spinney. As I see it, your job is straight uphill. The British have a strength that will smother you. And fighting with the Arabs of Palestine is a losing proposition, too." Newman voiced his doubts and continued. "But I love your determination and your die-hard people. Spinney and I are glad to have been with you."

The air was cold that evening, and Newman's sweater provided little warmth. Mrs. Simon wore only a summer jacket. "You must be terribly cold," he said.

"It is cold, but that is all right."

"Mrs. Simon, the only part of all this that bothers me is that your husband was a casualty. I guess I also mind that he had to be with people so inferior to him. That Marcus guy acted as though he were a king, above all the troubles that all the people of this place are suffering through."

"My husband was a messenger. He knew the dangers, but he loved the idea of helping people who really needed help. That was what drove him. These people may seem brave to you, Mr. Newman, but they are actually quite desperate. They have no one - no government to support them. No one. Just the faith that they are something, something larger than individuals, that they have a message. My husband respected just that - the message that he and these people represented."

"Marcus killed a part of that message. That act deserves a message, too." Newman looked up at the dark sky. The stars were covered by clouds.

"Take care, Mrs. Simon. Steady as she goes.

Steady as she goes."

The old lady looked up at him. "Go back to where you belong now. You have done enough for us. For a time I had hoped that you might stay here with us, worked on one of our farms, but I believe that none of this is right for you. I've wondered why you were not meant to stay with us, but I know you were not meant to do so. So be it. There are doubtlessly other plans that the Infinite One has in store for you. Go in peace and may the spirit of God go with you."

That was the last time that Newman saw Mrs. Simon.

****

"Another drink, Jake?" Spinney asked.

"Sure. Thanks. It'll warm me up. New England has a way of turning my insides into ice water. I don't know. Maybe I'm getting older faster than I think," Newman sighed.

Spinney filled his glass with whiskey straight up, and Newman took a mouthful.

"Never let a fellow drink alone, Jake. No sailor lets another sailor drink alone," and Spinney clicked his glass against Newman's.

Spinney was a barrel-chested man, different from the string-bean kid living in Newman's memory. Was this the kid who could run for a football or a baseball that seemed beyond anybody's reach? It was. Newman recognized the same humanity that exuded from his old friend even though his appearance had changed.

"Jim," Newman remarked, "no offense, but you sure do look like a cop. No kidding. You are the spitting image of a small town or big city detective. That tie and white shirt. Geez, you just naturally floated into this, didn't you?"

"I don't know, Jake. Maybe once I was made for this, but after fourteen years it's the same stuff, just a different day. Most of the time I just wonder how the day is going to get messed up or if I'm going to be the one that's going to ball it up. If I was made for this job, that was a while ago. Now I'm just another dinosaur waiting for some mud hole to slip into." Spinney filled Newman's glass and then filled his own.

Newman felt at ease sitting here overlooking a street that was big and hilly and deserted. This was a country house away from a town rapidly becoming a city.

"This house is a long way from the tenements of Suffolk Square. I want to know more about your wife and your kids," Newman asked.

"I have three of the greatest looking kids the good Lord provided. Two girls and a boy. My oldest, Mary, she's eleven. She's quiet and serious like her mother. She's a real good kid. Teddy is nine and can he hit a golf ball. A friend of mine got him a job caddying at a club and that led to his hitting a few on the side. That was all it took to get him hooked. I'm glad because he is one tough customer. A tough kid. I've given him a lot of rope, like my old man gave me. That boy needs my prayers. I hope the golf helps settle him down a bit; you know, get him on the right track and all."

"My little one, Amy, she's six going on eighteen. She's the one that keeps me young. She just doesn't let me get as planted in my chair as I'd like." It was obvious to Newman that Spinney enjoyed talking and thinking about his family, and Newman liked that.

A tall, thin woman with bright blue eyes, a smile, and long, dark hair came out on the porch. She wore a summer dress with what looked like her husband's sweater over it. "Jim, it's freezing in this house. Oh, I'm sorry, I didn't know you were with anybody."

"Oh this is more than anybody, Sharon. This is Jake Newman."

"Jake Newman. I've heard that name before, many times before. Jake Newman. You're the missing brother that Jim tells me he had. I doubted you even existed. My husband has told me many stories about you and the merchant marines and about your growing up together." She put her hand out and Jake held it, their smiles making it seem as though they had known one another for sometime.

"It's nice to meet you. It's nice to be in your house, too. Your husband and I are reminiscing a bit. I agree with you, it sure is cold. At one time I used to be able to put up with this New England weather, but that east wind makes life pretty cold even in summer. I had forgotten about that, but I'm remembering real quick." They all laughed.

Sharon's dark brown hair rested on her shoulders; her nose and mouth possessed a rather classic elegance. She was attractive and had an outdoors kind of glow that her presence carried into the indoors. She smiled so freely that Newman felt quite at ease.

"Jim was telling me about your children. It sounds like you have a nice life together. I used to know this part of town well, a while ago, of course, but this always was a nice place to raise a family."

"We love it here, and the kids do, too. Being here is like being away from everybody. The kids are great. I guess they are everything to us. But there's always something that rattles me or Jim. Usual stuff, I guess, usual in raising a family. But that's okay. There's no sense in getting too worked up about most things anyway." Sharon was a calming influence, Newman surmised. He could feel her easy manner.

"You guys get back to your talk. I don't want to bother you. But will you stay for dinner, Jake? I'd like you to meet the children."

"Thanks, but I do have plans this evening. Another time would be fine though."

"Whenever you're ready. We'll be here. Take care, Jake, and don't forget where we live." Giving a wave, she left the room.

"Nice, Jim. She seems real nice," Newman said with a sense of pleasure in his voice.

"Her entire family's that way. Nice folks," Spinney agreed

but with a sense of modesty. Jim was not one to show emotion, especially with those things that mattered. Over trivialities, he may have displayed emotion, but this was only feigned interest. For Jim, it was a survival skill. Spinney was a private person. He was old-time New England, having carved out his life from nothing other than the little that the earth gave of itself and his own willfulness.

Newman would have liked to say more about how much he liked the life Jim had made for himself, but he did not wish to embarrass his old friend. Jim did not allow such a conversation to occur.

"Jake, you're not back here just to visit. We both know that. But we know something else. There is nothing here for you ... nothing having to do with that night in Suffolk Square. Oh, I know it was awful, but it was awfully stupid. It is a part of that built in anti-Jewish attitude that we both have seen." Jim paused for a moment. Seeing that Newman wanted a part of the conversation, Jim stopped and took a sip from his glass.

"The world's going off the edge, old pal. Read the papers. And it isn't just Hitler and the Germans and that whole crew of fascists. Too many people who should know better are sitting by the wayside ... quiet, out of the way of any trouble. That's why I'm here. Somebody's got to care and turn a spotlight on this kind of stuff. That's all."

"Jake, I can understand that. But I know this town, and it isn't proud of that night ... no way."

Maybe it was the voice of his old friend or perhaps it was Spinney's savvy that Jake respected.

"I believe you, but the world says you're wrong. The world says that Gentiles, even old pals, cannot be trusted ... at least when it comes to Jews." Newman spoke without batting an eye.

"You don't believe that. I know I don't. You can't condemn all Christendom for ... for that kind of chicanery ... that's really what it is. It is a kind of never-ending chicanery that always fools the blessed morons of society." Spinney's response was in a still voice, but he did not back down from Newman's words.

"But I know one thing, Jake. Whoever sent you here had a sense of how fouled up life can be. If nothing else, I'm glad to see you." Jim raised his glass and said, "A toast to two kids from Suffolk Square ... the last of the Mohegans!"

"Absolutely!" Jake replied.

"You think I'm a sell out, don't you Jake?" Spinney smiled when he said this, and it caught Newman by surprise. "Jake, who's fooling who?"

"Come on, Jim, you went about your life. You got a job. Big deal, you got a job. So you're a cop, even the chief, so what." Newman remained surprised but not convinced that he even understood what Spinney meant.

"No. Not just that. It's coming back here to this place, ending up another working stiff like all the other assholes. And you're still stirring up one kind of trouble or another, like some knight or something, saving a damsel or pied-piping some damn rats into the ocean. You never stopped riding the trains or the boats or living in hotels. You never got the message."

"Jim ..."

"Jake, it is the truth. You never got the idea that you have to surrender. You have to give up, go about a life, settle into a life. I did that. Just settle into a life. But you never did, did you? You couldn't do that, could you? You couldn't trust anything long enough to do that." Spinney had said his piece.

"So, I'm the fool. I might surprise you yet. Maybe the sky is not going to fall in. I need a roof, too, Jim. You were constructive; you built something. Look at your kids and your wife and just the way every day starts up. Don't you think I could use that, too?"

Chapter Ten

Mr. Mayor

It was late in the afternoon when Newman left. He looked forward to the walk from the west side of town back to his hotel. Newman loved the old Victorian houses and the elm-lined streets. This genteel atmosphere was part of the attraction of small-town Massachusetts.

As his feet moved along the pavement, he noticed that some sidewalks were made of red bricks fitted into place, while others glittered with speckled-colored field rocks mixed with cement. The names of the contractors were etched into the sidewalks, as though the streets were artistic pieces that required a signature.

Fieldstone walls and pruned hedges framed some of the side yards. He admired the yards that contained a marble bench or lawn chairs that provided an inviting nature to the backyard. These were the dwellings of the comfortable. But even here, Newman noticed that times had changed. Once an exclusive preserve of the Protestant aristocracy, the town's premier neighborhood had been invaded by Malloys and Nolans. The land was subject to a new ethnic group and, doubtless, to the uniformly suspicious mentality that charac-terized so much of New England life.

Newman was no stranger to the charms of this town. He appreciated the architecture of the town's train station. The waiting room for the trains going to Boston was made of red sandstone with an enormous archway filled with small win-dow panes.

In the afternoon light, the glass glimmered a softness and serenity. The light gave an airy space for benches and high-backed wooden chairs.

The commuters wore either sweaters or light jackets. Clearly, the east wind was doing its job of providing New Englanders with a late afternoon.

He grew annoyed with his own introspection. "Let the weather simply be. Let it alone, and stop interfering," he thought. "Just live. Living is enough for you, however you wish to think of what enough means. Live. Let yourself alone. Let God alone. Get on with it. That is all that it takes. Forget whether it is cool or hot; forget the seasons; forget everything except that you are living. That is more than enough. Do not ask for more."

He became exasperated with himself. "You must stop trying to manage the weather. Enjoy the ride."

Now, Newman was in front of the Mystic Town Hall, a large, brick building that did not have the charm of so many of the other buildings in the town, but it had an enormous pitched roof which reminded him of an ancient schoolhouse. Etched in the wooden door of its entrance were two seals. One was of the Commonwealth of Massachusetts and the other of the town. On the town seal was a carved representation of the town common, used as a park just beyond the Congregational Church, and an outline of the Town Hall. Newman was relieved to enter the building and escape the afternoon sun.

The building's first floor seemed empty, and the enormous spiral staircase that ran to some higher level was also empty. Then Newman spotted a tiny fellow taking a drink from a water fountain to the left of the entranceway. The fellow was no taller than five feet two or three inches, and he had what appeared to be a bad leg. In fact, on his arm was a cane that was, of course, as large as a child's stick.

"Excuse me, I'm looking for the Mayor's office," Newman inquired.

The man turned toward Newman and wiped his lips. Some water dripped just where his shirt and tie converged. "Doesn't that happen all the time? You want his office. Well, up there near the Council Chamber is the Mayor's office, but you won't find him there. He's right here. I'm Gene Converse." Extended toward Newman was a hand that

Newman shook.

"I'm Jake Newman. I called your office and confirmed my appointment to see you today."

"I've been waiting for you, Mr. Newman. On a gorgeous day for gardening, it would take an appointment to find me indoors, but such are the demands of public office. I've looked forward to meeting with you. Let's avoid the stairs and go into the clerk's library. It's cool in there, and we will have some privacy. The Mayor led the way, and Newman observed the gentleman's legs, petite and somewhat bent, as they made their way through a series of doors where a variety of secretaries and clerks nodded to the Mayor and to Newman.

Amid rows of official-looking books entitled Census Records, Registry of Voters, and other enormous, bound volumes that Newman passed and fingered, they made their way to a wooden conference table. As they walked, the Mayor pointed out a picture on the wall or a particular title from the lined bookcases. The chairs, surrounding the conference table, provided the Mayor and Newman a place to sit down. It was obvious that the Mayor was relieved to place his cane on the back of his chair and let his small frame submerge into the seat.

"One of the benefits of a diminutive physical stature is that every chair provides a comfortable place to sleep. But you are not in the community to speculate on such things, that I know Mr. Newman. Not in the slightest."

"Mr. Mayor, I know that I am a guest here. But I also know that I am in town to understand what brought on the Suffolk Square riot and to make the people who live here feel secure about their lives."

"Quite understandable." Mayor Converse got up from his chair and without his cane he shuffled over to one of the bookcases.

"Mr. Newman, many people in town have tried to understand the troubles that the Suffolk Square area has experienced, and many of us regret what has occurred. But you are correct. To understand what happened is a bit more complicated." He sat back down into the chair, climbing almost to place himself squarely in the seat.

"I suppose I could tell you, first off, that I am the problem. Not me alone, I hope, but mayors before me as well. Families such as mine have dominated the life of this community. There are families, including mine, who own the mills, and the great rubber factory that is near the railroad lines, and all the other shops that are sprinkled throughout the area. Wealth and politics have a way of working together, Mr. Newman, to encourage those ideas that benefit the haves in our society. Often wealth and politics provide more than a single bully pulpit to promote all the self- congratulations that are required." The Mayor opened a large and seemingly heavy leaf of the book that was on the table in front of him.

"This book provides a kind of testimony to all that. It is a book that records where people live in town, where people work, how many children they have. We have maintained these records for over one hundred years. I often take a peek at them, and I have made a discovery that I knew to be true even before I looked at a dozen entries. This town has never produced a doctor, pharmacist, dentist, or even a successful businessman from the poorest wards of the town - the Irish wards and the black section of town. At least none of those people stayed in the town after they earned some success. And why should they? We all but drove people out.

The town wanted working backs and compliant muscles to labor in the factories but not to think. Do you know that no person from those areas even rose to be a manager or some other white-collar worker in our factories? Not one. For almost a hundred years if one were an Irishman, then it was the factory work-room where he would spend his working life. Maybe a woman might find herself in an office, upstairs beyond the furnaces and boilers, but that was for secretarial work. The plain fact of the matter was that the laboring people were to be exactly that. Anybody with ambition and ability from the Irish or other minority groups rapidly moved on out of here as fast as they could."

"You've got an Irish police chief," Newman observed.

"Our very first. His appointment raised all kinds of eyebrows, but, fortunately, the end of the world, which was predicted by some, did not occur."

The Mayor continued. "Mr. Newman, our national depression has changed certain sensitivities within the community, and President Roosevelt deserves some recognition for that. The Democrats have been reborn! Yet, it will be some time before prosperity and tolerance actually change a community, and maybe the entire nation. And in the meantime, all the simmering ignorance and bitterness pops from our collective past.

The Jews bring a unique opportunity for all bigots and for prejudice. It is ironic, I believe, that even our own Suffolk Square provides a geographical center for displaying how victimized we all become by intolerance. Mr. Newman, I make no excuses for what occurred. The legal system may explain what occurred one way; our churches may explain it another way; and maybe my explanations offer a third alternative. But it's all the same; only the extent of blame and guilt remain different. Victims, one and all, we are victims. I am a victim. And even you, sir, are a victim. Maybe when this community gets itself together, when it gets its confidence back, when the country gets its head back on, then maybe we can begin to change."

"And Suffolk Square ... why should the Jews of Suffolk Square be especially singled out?" Newman reflected.

"All the old businesses in town, the most established institutions, are interested in profits because it has been profits that have allowed the owners to boast of their wisdom. But when profits disappear, so do all the pretenses of infallibility. It is nearly religious. Why the Jews, you ask? Well, is there actually any answer that is not tied to some perversion of all that is human? The Jews are not as intimidated by failure or deflated by challenges to their wisdom. Suffolk Square is a beehive of energy and activity and, especially, of hope. There is extraordinary hope in that tiny neighborhood. We see it in politics and in the variety of community organizations. It is present in the schools. Hope is the lifeblood of the schools, and it is clear that there is a generation of children, many of whom are of your faith, who embody all that is hopeful. But this hope takes time for others to share. Suffolk Square will do fine, and I believe that the other neighborhoods in this tired town will also be rejuvenated. And there will be moments of despair and frustration and genuine unkindness. That is what we saw that night in Suffolk Square. It was a sadness. Victims, all victims, Mr. Newman. We must have sympathy for the victims!"

The Mayor was quiet. "It is hard for a mayor to lead such a change."

"And you, Mr. Mayor, how did you get into this business? Is the name Converse one of those established names you referred to?" Newman probed.

Getting to his feet, the Mayor laughed. "My father once told me that it was his view that a man of my physical stature needed to make a place in the world either in the circus or in politics. Politics would have me."

And for some time thereafter Newman listened as the Mayor talked.

****

167

Back in his hotel room, Newman, lying on his bed, closed his eyes and believed that his feet knew every step he had taken to Suffolk Square from Spinney's house. He lifted his head high on the pillow that was too hard for him and thought of tossing it on the floor by the bed. He was too relaxed to move. His breathing began to invade his mind then to escape his attention. He slept, but even his sleep was not free from pain.

Images pursued him. High grasses filled an enormous field of wheat. He heard Yiddish. Some voices were known to him: the voice of his mother, his father, a lady who had lived down the street. What was everyone doing in this field?

Other voices were unfamiliar. Some spoke in another tongue. He did not understand a word.

Suddenly, there was terror in the voices, and the words were in English. "Quick. Quick. Move fast for they will be here, and you must get away from here. Go to the forests and keep going. Just keep going. Hide anywhere you can, under the leaves and the branches of the bushes. Quick. Don't you understand? They will beat you. Maybe even kill you. Go. Go. Now before they come here." Voice after voice repeated the same words. "Run! Run! Quickly."

But the warnings were of no use. Newman's feet could not move. It was if he were planted, like a common plant or tree stump. He could not get his feet to move.

"I cannot run away from here. Why should I run from anybody? This is my home. I belong to this place. My friends live here; my family has called this our home; we have lived here for five hundred years. No one will allow any harm to come to me. We are the same people; we all call this place ours; no one can say otherwise." And Newman's thoughts were planted into his mind and heart, so planted that the ground around him would not allow him to move even if he had so desired. And these thoughts kept his feet in place, not allowing escape.

But then Newman looked at a body on the ground, a body clothed in khaki pants and a blue shirt, and the body was Newman's body, dressed exactly as he was dressed. Looking down at himself, strewn on the ground and surrounded by the high grass, there was a wound on the side of his head and a larger bloody wound around his right shoulder. The body was motionless except for breathing.

"I lie here? How can this be? Who struck me and why?"

"Who struck me?" Newman shouted for all to hear. Surely, someone could hear him. Again, his voice called out, "Who struck me?"

But there was only quiet and stillness. There was not a sound. Neither was there wind or air, heat or cold, but only the reverberation of the words, "Who struck me?"

"This must be my death. That is what this must be. This must be my end," thought Newman, his eyes looking for any sign but seeing just a large grassy plain. "I thought I knew this place. But do I?"

His ears were alert to even a whisper, any sound that might explain where he was. Newman looked up from the ground, away from the body that was his, and he was alone.

Then, the body on the ground began to rustle and move as though there was someone rousing it. Newman appeared to hear something, as though both the figure on the ground and he, standing, had been awoken from a sleep. He heard a slight but high pitched cry, the cry of a cat, but there was no such creature to be seen. And then Newman heard something else.

He saw a small, quite thin black cat walk near the body on the ground and, as though the skinny creature was an inch from his head, Newman heard the cat purr. And the

purring grew louder and louder to the extent that the sound
was a whirlwind, an engine, a motor of a sound. And then
the sound and the cat were gone, gone into the grass just as
bizarrely as when the creature first appeared.

As Newman looked all about him, he was aware that he
was the person on the ground and that he was no longer
looking at himself, or that he had been separated from himself. Newman stirred from the ground and sat up, touching
his head. And then there was a wind, a wind that blew
warmly.

****

Sharon was putting dishes into a large, white cupboard
that had glass-covered doors and glass-knobbed handles.
Everything was neatly stacked, and each of the children had
a small chore to perform before three whacking sounds of the
back porch screen door announced that early evening play-
time had begun. Sharon noticed a decided distance in her
husband's mood, the kind of aloneness into which he slid in
those moments when uncertainty reigned supreme. Even as
chief, the politics of town government were a part of every
year's budget battles. Unemployment wrecked havoc in
household after household, and that was before the black
days of the depression. The fact was that as poor paying as a
policeman's lot was, it was equally short on security.

Jim may have had that twinkle of insecurity in his eyes
before, but this was different. And Sharon tried to decipher
what was wrong.

"Too bad your old pal couldn't stay. But he'll be about,
won't he?" she gently asked.

"Oh, I think so. I'm glad he came by. It is just like when
we were kids. The same good guy, just older and probably
just as stubborn. What's that old saying: great to see you,

170

great to see you on your way."

"Come on now. I was happy to meet him. What's he doing? Going to write some newspaper articles? This town could care less, what with all the horror stories already in the papers." Sharon kept putting glasses and large supper plates in their places.

Jim walked about the kitchen, looking out the window, spotting Amy hanging upside down from a swing that was about three or four feet off the ground. "Look at that Amy. God, does she scare me when she's on that swing. That kid spends more time upside down than rightside up. Can somebody actually walk on their head? When I look at her out there I wonder.

Jake was, and I think still is, some kind of knight. An older knight than when we were in the merchant marines, but even then he was getting himself into all kinds of things ... politics, Jewish this or Jewish that ... I've forgotten all the little errands into the wilderness. But that was Jake. That was more than Jake. It was what mattered, and it mattered to me, too. For some reason, neither he nor I could walk away from things ... like what happened in Suffolk Square. That was awful, but then is not now. But to him it is. That is what bugs me. I know him. What happened there was something ugly, and he's going to hold it up to anybody whose nose is nearby."

"Does that bother you? You aren't responsible for what happened. Those boys aren't the only bad apples around here, but they're a bunch of nobodies." Sharon tried to help, and Jim sensed that in her words and in her voice.

"Listen, I know that. And I hope Jake does, too. But it happened. It happened here, in this town that he and I were born in. Stuff like that drives him a bit daffy, and that's why I'll be just as glad when he leaves."

But Spinney was not through with what was on his mind.

171

Sharon could feel the restlessness as he moved from one chair to another or simply to lean against a counter.

Sharon waited for her husband to put the right words to his emotions. "Jake has a dark view of people, almost as though he merely waits for the negatives or the flaws in a person to make it to the surface ... sort of just waiting, waiting for a person to open themselves up. I've seen it before, when we were in one place or another. And I felt a little of that today. He's easy-going; that's what you might think. But he's not really easy. He's waiting and watching, like he's playing cards and expecting a certain card to fall into his hand. And when it does, it wouldn't surprise him. Maybe that's one of the things I never saw before but now I see. He expects screw ups. He expects to be let down, and I felt that from him. If I had turned out to be some crazy ugly person, maybe somebody who wanted to see those people in Suffolk Square get their butts kicked, well, that wouldn't have fazed him. He expects to be let down, to be disappointed, and especially by people he knows. I don't know how to explain it. He expects that people will act like chickens, and they usually do. But, Jesus, he expected it of me, too."

"I think you're reading too much into it. He seems like a real friendly guy, and he's a friend. Maybe he's just doing his job ... just like you do your job."

"Doing our jobs is one thing. Being friends and doing our jobs is another. Sharon, that guy is not an easy guy. He's no maniac or anything ... just what I said though. He's got a case of the darkness ...

And there's plenty around here that's worthy of darkness. The damn depression has sucked whatever spunk people may have had. People are leaving this place in droves, and nobody's fool enough to live around here by choice. Factories closing down ... politics is like some constant death struggle between the rich and the mighty and the might-have beens.

172

Honestly, has the country ever seemed more like it's going to just up and die? And then those delinquents who went berserk in Suffolk Square! You know as well as I do - and don't think old Jake isn't going to think it, too - that kind of stuff happens when the factories lay off and when the loons are on the lookout for the most convenient devil. There's enough darkness around here for a nationwide blackout." Jim wasn't finished with his thought, but he was exhausted.

But now Jim headed out the backdoor. Soon, Sharon heard Amy squeal with delight, and then she heard her husband say, "How do you hang upside down by your toes? Show me how I can do it!"

And Amy's voice came into the kitchen by the window over the kitchen sink. "Mommy, daddy's going to hurt himself again. Mommy ..."

Chapter Elven

Pity the Wisdom of Jake Newman

Ginsburg opened a large, oak door down from the main corridor of the hotel. Newman noticed that the oak door dwarfed Ginsburg, who was limping.

"Mr. Ginsburg, is something wrong with your leg?" Newman asked.

"Ah, Mr. Newman, there is something wrong with an old man every day. Today it is my leg ... maybe it is my back, too. Maybe I picked something up wrong. Who can say? My doctor tells me to be more careful. My guests tell me to get their bags. Who is one to listen to?"

"I know the problem," Newman laughed.

"Enough of me. This is where your meeting can be held. It will be quiet, and you can have some refreshments. What did you say? Four or five people?"

"Yes. No more than five. You probably know them." Newman read from his notebook. "Mr. Joruchoff, the attorney; Miss Aronoff, the daughter of the baker; Mr. Zeitler and Jason Machinkoff, two elderly gentlemen who were injured in the Square; and Mr. John Tucker, a black man from one of the oldest families in the town." He closed his notebook. "If we could have coffee or tea, that would be fine."

"No problem. What do you think of this room?"

"Wonderful. The floor looks like no one has walked on it, and the wainscotting is incredible."

"I'm glad you like it. This room was part of the house that the hotel was built around. That was long before I owned it. The house was built by a man named Barrett, an eccentric Harvard professor. He must have been well-to-do because he left his position and took up residence here. This whole area used to be fields and marsh land stretching to the sea. He owned all of it. He had been married at one time, and he even had children. When he moved into the house, he came alone, and he stayed in the house for twenty years. Why he did this, no one knows. I have heard that he was interested in the marshes but not interested in students or his family."

Newman admired Ginsburg's knowledge of history and

people. "What about this room, Mr. Ginsburg?" Newman asked.

"This room? Well, Barrett had this room, which he used as a dining room, built to exact specifications. Moldings and flooring, all of the wood, were brought from Boston, and the carpenters themselves were brought in from New Hampshire. He wanted peace and a beautiful room in which to eat. When I bought the place, after he had died, the entire house was in considerable disrepair. I took some care to restore the gentleman's room. Now, every time I come into the room, I am reminded of him and, rightly or not, how he tried to bring peace to his life."

"Mr. Ginsburg, thanks for letting me use it. And thanks for the story, too."

Later that evening, the chairs that surrounded the honey-colored table in the center of Mr. Ginsburg's great room were occupied. Newman presided.

He began abruptly. "I am not here to tell you folks what to do. I said this to all of you when we first met. Yet you and others have told me that there is some business that remains to be done. Some display of your frustrations needs to be shown. I have thought about this, and I have learned much from so many people in the community. Also, I have received some instructions from my superiors as to what the community might consider."

Newman realized that their reaction to his suggestions was going to be a test both for him and the community. Perhaps it was assumed that without Newman's leadership, the community would simply ignore its hurt. Perhaps if Newman suggested little in the way of redress, the community may allow it all to slip into the past. But all at the table understood that that was not to be. Instead they listened, somehow knowing they were receiving a plan that would benefit them all.

"We are going to engage in a vigil," Newman resumed, "a vigil that will last for forty miles. Our vigil will pay witness to our shared concerns about our rights, our freedom, and our feeling that intimidation cannot be tolerated, even intimidation disguised as anger. We will not tolerate being beaten by some people and ignored by others." Newman stopped to note the faces of the group seated before him.

"You represent the larger community. And it is clear to me that the community is not interested in punishment as much as it is interested in telling itself something. The community wants to tell itself that it is safe and free. That is fine, but first the community needs to tell itself that it is a community. When one group experiences pain, the entire community needs to cry out that the pain must stop. When some people in the community, regardless of their color or religion or where they may have come from, when people fear for their children, fear for the havoc that violence plays in people's hearts, then all people need to rise up and parade through the city. We are going to demonstrate this fact. We are going to get parade permits, and we are going to walk forty miles from Suffolk Square through all the neighborhoods of this town."

"We are going to parade and bear witness to demonstrate who we are. What we learn from this event will tell us about ourselves, our friends, and our enemies, too. But I want you to know something; your feet will conquer your fear. The key to making people understand your pain is to let this whole community, this whole country, see your faces ... and watch your feet ... and see, again, your faces. Seeing will make all the fear disappear, and it will show people that the human face is remarkably alike, remarkably similar to the human spirit. We can do this. We can show ourselves that we can do this."

Newman said what he felt needed to be said, and he felt that whatever the consequences of his words, or the actions that would follow, required that he prepare himself and the group that listened.

"Do you expect to have many people participate in this,

Mr. Newman?"

"Will children march?"

"What about those who do not wish to participate?"

"Will the police grant us a permit?"

"Will we need protection?"

"Will we march through the night?"

"People will not accept such a plan."

"Some people will follow."

"What will be proven from such an idea?"

"Why forty miles? What's so special about forty?"

"Who will lead us? Where will the march start? Where will it end?"

Questions swirled about Mr. Barrett's peaceful dining room. Jake Newman patiently answered them, one by one, stopping long enough to move about the room giving everybody an opportunity to voice a concern or make an observation. In the end, the group accepted Newman's plan, but the group did not possess Newman's sense of what the march might accomplish.

Newman had little problem accepting the group's uncertainty. He understood that the march needed to occur, regardless of the limitations of support or faith in its goals. So it goes, Newman thought. The event will either convince them or it will not. That is as it should be, Newman concluded.

****

About a dozen individuals worked on organizing the forty-mile demonstration. The local press and the Boston press were alerted, and a host of commentators speculated on the usefulness of the demonstration. During the first week of organizational meetings, elderly people, many of whom had been affected by the assault in Suffolk Square, signed up to march. Those who had been injured would wear bandages on the day of the march as a sign of the distress caused by the

180

violence.

In the evenings there were meetings held in Newman's hotel, or in someone's kitchen, or in a corner of the delicatessen. Newman attended every meeting and afterwards slipped back to his hotel room to type his report that was then picked up by a number of news services. The headlines became part of the summer's calendar, just as some of the winning or losing baseball scores become an obsession for at least a while. Newman, too, found each day filled with this obsession.

"You have really messed up all the people in this town, not just a few Irish kids who called Jews `Christ Killers'. You have screwed up this town for everybody." Such was Michael's harangue. "A few kids act goofy, and the whole crazy photographic world is alerted to snap pictures of old ladies and their grandchildren walking the streets like gypsies. What are you proving?"

Newman tried to sympathize with Michael, but he couldn't. Michael, who was well-dressed with polished shoes, expensive suits and shirts, was ambitious for even greater wealth and power. Newman learned that he and his family owned over twenty percent of the rental property in town and was endlessly speculating in building all kinds of houses and storefronts. His ambition did not bother Newman. However, when his ambition conflicted with the community's well-being and dignity, that was the point where Michael compromised the community's interests.

That bothered Newman. It bothered him that Michael accepted the little intimidations, even violence, so that business could go on. Newman felt that there was something tormented about Michael's cynicism. "Maybe people like Michael were right for five thousand years of Jewish survival, but that kind of survival will get you no where in America. Struggle and let everyone witness your struggle - that's the only way to stand up for your rights. You've got rights, you know. You've got rights. That's what's different about Michael and me. He's playing by the rules of an old and woefully flawed game."

"You think this is your wisdom, don't you?" Newman said to himself. "This is the wisdom that got you punished as a kid, the kind of wisdom that cried out like a street kid: 'come on, let's go, you found your fight'. Even if there are a thousand Mystics, a thousand skirmishes between Jews and all who torment them, even if all of those struggles took him from one end of America to the other, it would be worth it. It would be worth living on a merry-go-round as long as the message gets out that all the old-world excuses for persecuting Jews will no longer work."

"Michael, tell me," Newman said, "these kids who screamed 'Christ Killers', who are they? They're kids. Only kids. But they learned to hate somewhere. And we want that hate to stop. All that we are going to do is let people know that the violence stops here. Let's kill all the myths before the myths kill us. That's the end of the story. Maybe we will get the message across, maybe we won't. But that is the message. Do you have a problem with that, Michael?"

"I plan on living in this town long after you are a memory. Don't talk to me about my problems. I have a stake here. My family belongs here. It is the problem of the have and the have nots. I happen to be one of the haves."

"Other people in the town have a stake ..."

Michael interrupted. "They have nothing. What have they got? Their lives. That is it. And by the way, don't go leading my wife around either. She spends more time planning the walk around this town than she does in her own bed. Maybe that's part of the difference between the haves and the have nots, too."

"Your wife's one of the planners of this effort. She has certain values. Does that make her a have not?"

"Let's put it this way, Newman. Ever since I met you, I knew you were trouble. You're trouble for me anyway. Let Rebecca decide for herself what she wants to do. If marching

182

around town is what she wants to do, she's part of the trouble, too." Michael turned to go, then turned to face Jake.

"At least we know one thing about you," he sneered. "You show up for the funerals."

****

Walking back to his hotel, he seethed with an anger so great that he could only think about bashing Michael with his fists. "I'd like to smash those words into the earth," he thought, realizing that his passions mattered to him. It was as though he had finally learned something about himself. He cared. This was something that mattered to him.

Back at the hotel, somewhat calmed because of his fast-paced walk, he scolded himself. "Do the job you are supposed to do," he mumbled.

Catching sight of himself in the mirror, he noticed that his face looked weary and old. "You are looking more and more like a worn-out pocketbook," he told himself. Newman slept the better part of the afternoon and into the night. He dreamed no dreams. He possessed only the strength to stretch out his limp body and then close his eyes, hoping that nature would satisfy his need for rest.

****

The next day, Newman met with the Walking Brigade, as they called themselves. Twelve individuals sat in the last few tables of the Suffolk Square delicatessen. Their leader was Milt Kriensky, a man in his sixties with a silver-knobbed walking stick. His slicked-back, gray hair suggested that in his youth he had been handsome. Now he was a patriarch of the community. Planning the march gave him a sense of purpose.

"We must march through the Linden neighborhood," Kriensky advised.

The others nodded. The Linden section had a history of excluding Jewish residents. "We will walk through the center of the Linden neighborhood quietly and respectfully, then head for the Linden Commons for a prayer and a few words by certain dignitaries. Then we shall turn around and proceed to walk through the seven wards of the town and around the entire town. We will walk forty miles. There will be some who will march the entire distance, but we expect to be helped by others who wish to join us for part of the walk. The town is about 22 miles around and inch-by-inch we will walk it. We will sing as we walk. Then we will enter Suffolk Square, sometime on Sunday evening ... God only know's what time! But whenever it is, we shall get there and there will be more singing, so much singing that the entire town will not be able to sleep. So much singing that our voices will be heard across this state, across the country. President Roosevelt will hear our singing, and he will be inspired by our voices! Only then will we be content. Only then will we be satisfied."

Newman took care in selecting the individuals that met in Mr. Ginsburg's dining room. Mrs. Dennehey, Miss Donovan, and Mrs. DePauer, all members of the Edgeworth Irish-American Society, had been introduced to him by Chief Spinney. Well-educated, mature women interested in their community and their church, they were outraged by the events in Suffolk Square and wanted to express their support. And in all the discussions and meetings that were held, they devoted their time and energies in a manner that Newman admired.

The press was represented by Mr. Tim Leahy, the editor of the *Edgeworth Citizen*, and a young reporter, Frank Callahan, who took notes diligently.

A black Baptist minister, Reverend Earl Henson, articulated the concerns of his congregation. "The members of our church have never let a decent cause down. That's what our church and every church is about. A good cause brings out the fairness in people. Anyway, there are duties to be done and many of us are some of the senior residents in this town, and we know more than most what is fair and what is not. We'll be there."

Newman recorded the faces and expressions of all his guests. Mr. Robert Bertini of the Italian-American League was short and wide and looked every bit the way Newman supposed a mason should look. Two young brothers, John and Jeffrey Lyons, were members of the local Congregational Church; two young women, Maria Aly and Mrs. Felicity Lenan, were teachers who had contacted Newman about the second week he had arrived in town. They volunteered to help him in whatever way they could.

"Maria and I are far from the only teachers and parents in town who are delighted to teach eager and willing pupils," Mrs. Lenan explained, her long arms gesturing with every word.

When everyone was seated and Mr. Ginsburg had closed the door, Newman talked with them.

"It is not our goal to point any fingers at people. Our goal is to help ourselves bear witness to the voice of tolerance and respect and to speak out against injustice. So this demonstration, what somebody called the "Walking Brigade", wants to welcome all of you as participants!"

"On the fourth Sunday in August we want all those interested in participating to use the three roads that lead to Suffolk Square. The march will go around the town, slowly and steadily, without any disorderliness. I figure that the march will be something like forty miles. That should provide plenty of exercise and plenty of public recognition for our cause. As long as people hear the name Suffolk Square, we want them to remember what we did. We are going to walk this town, and we are going to help one another do it. Everybody is going to help everybody. We know we can't change the world. We know that in Europe wherever Hitler goes, people will be in danger and live in fear. But in

America we are walking ..."

"... and singing," someone shouted out.

"... and singing. Walking and singing and bearing witness to our rights and our belief in our right and everybody's right to live in peace. To live without fear, and to live without apologizing for who we happen to be. That's it in a nutshell. Some people may call us crazy, but that's all right. Those folks can say what they want. They don't realize how good walking is for one's health and for one's mind. So we need to show them. We'll show people that walking and singing can raise spirits. That's what we're going to do. Walk. Walk and sing for forty miles. Folks, old and young, are going to let their feet talk for them and tell everyone who sees us or hears us that we were not afraid to walk, any more than we are afraid to stand up for our rights. That is it. That is all we are about. And thank God that we have folks like you who are willing to go for long walks."

****

There was a wild kind of cheering as people showed up for the marathon of walking events, and there were plenty of people in the Square. Ginsburg estimated that two hundred people were in the Square, but soon that number doubled as women showed up pushing carriages, and the entire children's choir of the Baptist Church were there, dressed in their choir outfits. The streets were jammed with people, all milling about the center of the town. Even some of the local politicians showed up. But most folks were less concerned with who was there than with the simple fact that there were so many people there. There was a loud, boisterous conviviality to the gathering, not solemn or especially onerous considering what lay ahead of the group. But that suited Newman fine, and he was not in the least surprised at the turn out.

It drizzled the morning of the march as the crowd assembled on the sidewalks of Suffolk Square. Umbrellas were everywhere, almost a kind of sea of umbrellas. It was an enormous gathering of old men holding the hands of their grandchildren. Old women lifted their umbrellas over their heads. The drizzle gave way to a light summer rain.

A member of one of the synagogues read a prayer in Hebrew. He then translated the prayer into English. Reverend Henson said a few words, and he read a prayer, too. And then the march began.

Beckah helped with every tiring step. Her husband was absent, but her daughter Sarah walked beside her. Scores of other young people were there - high-school age people whose presence was like a ray of light. Newman noticed these people and could not help but think of the power of youth, the extraordinary contribution that youth brings to any effort. Those eager faces and bright eyes possessed a rightness and affirmation.

Newman glanced at his watch. Ten fifty. Nearly four hours had passed since the march had begun. People peered out of their windows.

The hours passed. The cloud-filled sky sprinkled rain through the filter of the trees and overhanging branches. The rain lightly showered the marchers as though it were an outpouring of confetti. And the movement of the people brought a sense of life to the daylight hours, and people's voices provided further testimony that the feet of the people could in fact speak for them, could reveal a sense of caring.

But it was the spectacle of it all, an honest spectacle of intriguing proportions that gave way to spontaneous chattering, which then gave way to voices in song. At moments, even the silence of the group made one strain to see and listen for, perhaps, an imperceptible sound.

People watching from the windows above the street applauded and whistled at the marchers. Some people shouted and waved to individuals whom they recognized.

Some people had their window shades pulled down tightly. In other windows residents peered out to see the marchers but said nothing. There were stares.

There is something about the nature of people that any time two or three hundred people assemble an identity of the crowd emerges. It's as though every crowd has a configuration as to its mood and pulse. Despite the dampness of the day, Suffolk Square possessed a sense of expectation and almost high adventure, as though the act of circumnavigating the town brought people together and made people rediscover the town and themselves.

Newman had no guarantee that the collective presence of the marchers was anything but an expression of witness, of people's attempt to participate in an event that was a positive statement that peace, brotherhood, and freedom were meant to convey. "Is this the closest I will get to a miracle?" Newman wondered.

Newman longed for a miracle. Newman had never experienced even the most transient of miracles, and his heart cried out for some resolution, some lasting sign that the crowd's fervor for human goodness might be realized. But the crowd itself was the miracle. That was the only answer that Newman could believe.

****

December, 1928 ...

"Human goodness," Newman murmured. The thought reminded him of the limitations of those words. He recalled the smugness of Marcus extorting money from all the freedom fighters in Palestine, using his British associations to live out his fantasy of being the overseer of helpless Arabs and Jews.

He remembered his conversation with Spinney, and his plan to show that intimidation was evil. "We're going to teach that fellow what it means to suck air, Jim," was the way he had put it.

And Spinney understood. He knew the dark side of Newman, the side that needed a struggle and a fight It was the "street kid" in Newman, Spinney thought, the kid that defended his turf against all takers. Spinney shared both the streets and the mentality.

"Jake, that son-of-a-bitch deserves a fate even we can't give him," Spinney responded with anger. He looked up, paused, and then with hope in his voice, concluded with the words that he knew Jake wanted to hear. "But we could sure try."

"Exactly. We know Marcus is not worth getting killed over because that would let you down, me, Mrs. Simon, and the merchant marines. But there is a message that he needs to receive. Maybe it'll shake his cage. Maybe he'll kill himself for us."

Newman began to explain what Marcus was in store for. Two days later the plan unfolded.

Marcus' butler answered the ring. With a thick accent that was German or Austrian, he asked, "Who is there, bitte? What is it that you want?"

"We have a package for Mr. Marcus," Spinney answered in a robust voice.

"Who are you?"

"We are seamen aboard the American ship, Delaware Shore, and we have a package that is to be delivered personally to Mr. Marcus."

"Leave it by the door."

"Sorry, sir, our instructions were to deliver the package only to Mr. Marcus."

"Leave it by the door. Herr Marcus will take your package at a later time."

"Pardon us, sir," Newman added, "but we cannot do that. Our orders are to place the package in Mr. Marcus' hands and that's the only way the package will remain here. Get

Mr. Marcus to take the package."

Thirty seconds went by.

A British voice was heard. "Yes, what is it? You have something for me?" Dressed in a cardigan sweater over a collared shirt and a bow tie, Marcus opened the door.

"This is from Mr. Simon, sir. He said you would be expecting it." Spinney held out the package in its brown wrapper.

Marcus drew back. "What do you mean? Simon? Is this some sort of a joke? Who are the two of you?" Clearly, Simon's name had disconcerted the British customs inspector.

"Seamen, sir. Mr. Simon asked us to drop this off to you. He was on our ship a ways back, but this is our first chance to make it here. Here you are, sir."

"Max, take that and show these gentlemen to the gate."

But before the doorman could carry out this order, Newman said, "Sir, Mr. Simon said that we would receive ten pounds for the delivery."

"Can you imagine!" Marcus exploded. With disgust, he reached into his pocket and pulled out a billfold from which he counted out the ten pounds.

The sailors disappeared as Max carried the package to a nearby table. Marcus opened the wrapper and untied a string. Inside the box was a small, metal tin with a difficult lid. With the aid of a knife, Max finally pried the lid open. Coiled within was a heap of yellow straw. Cautiously Marcus looked through the straw, then tipped the can upside down to assure himself that nothing else was inside.

"What?" he remarked, exasperated that his time and energies had been wasted. "Max, I have an appointment, and this business is making me late." His energy now redirected, Marcus' voice sped with orders. "Never admit those men again. Drive me to Colonel Quinn's house. Quick. Just lock up, and, yes, you may have the rest of the evening. Can you believe it ... friends of Simon. Hoodlums. That's what they are. Get the car! I have to be somewhere."

Neither Marcus nor Max were aware that Spinney had all the time he needed during the discussion of the package's delivery to do a little work. He filled the door locks with a soft putty which would prevent the door from locking. The door would appear to be locked, but with the assistance of a long, right-angle turning key, the lock could quite easily be unlatched.

"This will do nicely," Jim explained. "The putty will prevent the lock from slipping into its mechanism, and then I will lift its bar and presto ... we will be honored guests in his house."

****

Accompanied by his wife, Marcus returned to his home later in the evening. Marcus was slightly drunk.

As soon as he entered, Marcus felt uneasy and began to go from room to room. He surveyed the living room. Not a piece of furniture had been disturbed. He went into his bedroom before his wife had even entered the front door. Yellow straw was piled up on the king-size bed and knee-deep on the floor. Marcus was amazed. Suddenly, his wife shrieked from the hallway. She had opened a closet, and yellow straw had flowed out over her feet.

"What is this?" his wife gasped. She entered the kitchen. "Marcus, look at this place. And it smells like a stable!" she cried in fright. The kitchen and the sitting-room to its left were knee-deep in yellow straw. Their European-style home had become a barn.

"Those sailors! They are responsible for this. They did this." And without stopping to comfort his alarmed wife, Marcus ran to his car, put it in gear, and sped toward the docks.

The lights of the Delaware Shore were reflected in the water. Marcus jumped out of his car, ran up the gangplank, and down the walkway onto the deck of the ship. It was deserted on the main deck. He opened a door and walked below deck to a lit corridor and a room where three sailors sat at a table with playing cards spread out in front of them.

"Look who is here. Marcus, you've come. How nice," Spinney offered, smiling at the disheveled man before him. "Like a drink?"

"Who are you? What do you want?" Marcus was out of breath. His eyes were blazing, and his face was flushed a deep red.

"Jake, who is this guy?" asked Angelo Sabbatino, a member of the crew who was addicted to gin rummy.

"Sorry, Angelo. I thought everyone knew Inspector Marcus of the British Customs Authority in Palestine. Inspector Marcus, this is Angelo Sabbatino from Providence, Rhode Island, and one of the better card players in the merchant marines of the United States." Jake nodded to Angelo recognizing his friend's preeminence.

Marcus scoffed and repeated, "For the last time, what are you up to?"

"Dear Marcus, the honorable inspector, whatever is it that you are talking about?"

"You swine. You're pushing me. You know what I'm talking about. What are you up to? Do you think you are going to treat me like the vermin on this ship?"

"Marcus, Marcus ... no need to get excited. What's the problem? Some straw find its way into your home? So what? We thought you would want something like straw to remind you of your humble origins ... or at least our humble origins. It has worked, too. You want to know more about the straw, but we wanted to get your attention and to tell you how rotten it was to turn your back on people ... the way you did to your pal, Mr. Simon. Right? Mr. Simon, the old American gentleman who padded your pocket. We want you to think about how badly you treated him," Jake answered still sipping his drink.

"Simon? He was a smuggler. What business is that of

yours? Are you smugglers ... or maybe you're just a bunch of Jews, too."

With this assessment, Marcus pulled a revolver from the pocket of his jacket and pointed it at Newman.

"Marcus, wait a second. You aren't about to shoot American sailors, are you? Aboard their ship? Unarmed? Playing cards?" Jake questioned with extreme politeness.

"Who do you think would care? Who is going to care about a bunch of corrupt sailors ... smuggling arms and Jews into Palestine? That is your game. Who is going to give a damn about people like you?"

"Hold on, Marcus. I happen to be one-hundred percent Irish-American, and I resent any other identification," Spinney remarked. "Smuggling is something different. Smuggling is a hobby. Right, Jake?"

"That sounds about right to me. But I must admit something so that Marcus understands. I am not Irish, and I'm not Anglo-Saxon either. No, I am one of those Jews you're talking about, Marcus. And I don't mind telling you that my family will certainly be upset if something happens to me.

"Right, Jake. One or two other people might be upset, too."

"Bloody fools. I am not amused by you or your straw or your company. You are in for an education."

A loud voice interrupted what was occurring in the room. "Who called me a nigger? I heard somebody call me a nigger."

Into the room appeared an extended arm, a black arm, and attached to its hand was a Colt 45 with an enormous barrel, cocked and pointed at the head of Marcus.

"Was it you?" the voice rang out, shattering all other conversation and concerns.

Marcus turned to find his nose lined up into the barrel of the firearm.

"You better drop that gun. I mean to talk to you."

Marcus dropped the gun gently on the cardtable. Spinney

picked it up from the table and started unloading its ammunition.

Jake gestured to Marcus. "This is first-mate Jefferson, and he is touchy about people calling him names of a racial nature. He is an excellent shot, too, so I concur with your decision to put your gun on the table."

Jefferson removed his revolver from Marcus' nostrils but did not put the revolver too far from sight.

"Did your wife ask about the straw?" Jake asked. "It was our way of reminding you that people, at least where we are from, do not like bullies, and it is wrong to treat people as though they are slaves, alive only to spin straw for princesses or make bricks for Pharaoh. Do you get it Marcus? Here we are in Palestine and you're still treating people as though they are fit only to trample on straw."

"Does your wife recognize how you have been plundering the pockets of Jews and the Arabs around here? Does she suspect that you are a bully, Marcus? Perhaps you can explain our actions to her when she asks why her lovely home looks like a barn." Marcus was not interested in his wife's reaction.

"Are you going to kill me?" he demanded.

"Oh, no. Kill you? No. We are going to make you swim a bit though." With that remark, the ship's horn gave out a warning blast, and the engines shifted into gear. Slowly, very slowly, the ship was getting underway.

****

Soon afterwards, Marcus could be seen swimming back to the dock as the merchant marine vessel rippled over some waves and sliced through others on its way to the deep sea. Within sight of land, maybe a quarter of a mile from shore, Marcus was still making his way to shore.

Newman smiled as he remembered how Spinney and he had enjoyed the sight of the rotund Englishman thrashing his arms through the warm and deeply green waters.

****

People were watching the marchers from their windows, from porches, from the hillside, and from their front steps. Despite all the talk and preparation for the walk, some people looked out their windows wondering what it was all about and even who the marchers were.

"Jews from Suffolk Square. The whole lot of them."

"What the hell! What about those other folks? Every Negro in the damn town is in the line behind them. And Mrs. Aly and her tribe, too. What's going on here?"

Pouring into the three thoroughfares that led into Suffolk Square were lines of moving people, talking or singing, or just saying nothing ... sometimes quiet and dignified but apparently quite wet.

So it went. Through the evening, the marchers walked.

****

Four tables had been placed in front of the Converse Hotel, clearly the work of Mr. Ginsburg.

Eliott Mahlman, a lawyer in town, spoke first. "Friends, fellow citizens," he began, "hurrah for you and hurrah for justice. This is a celebration for decency. Here in the rain you have proven that the goal of goodness can be a powerful force. Every step of the way could only have happened because you wanted goodness to be king in this town!"

Mahlman's words brought applause from the crowd. While the cheers continued, he helped someone join him on the stage. For a moment the newcomer's identity was unclear. Then a female voice began.

"Ladies and gentlemen, ladies and gentlemen, my name is Beckah Collier. Like a lot of you, I wondered what this march would accomplish. I wasn't sure whether it was a

195

good idea or just another way to keep people apart. But today I see that this march has been more than good. This day has been extraordinary. I wish this whole country could know about this march, because it has reaffirmed what is special about our country - our respect for people's rights and a respect for all people. For forty miles we have marched to show support for one idea - that nobody needs to be afraid because of their religion or race. We have a right to decide for ourselves what matters to us. We have a right to let the town know that speaking our minds is another right that we have."

The audience clapped in agreement.

Beckah continued, "I was one of those people who wanted to let time make me forget that people in my town had been ill-treated. It took me more time than most of you not to be afraid of speaking out against that treatment. But you encouraged me. The march today helped me realize that being afraid is like dying. To be alive is to have hope and to help one another. You've made this day special. Suffolk Square will never be the same because of this day."

A forceful applause broke out as Beckah was helped from the stage. Mr. Joruchoff then reached down from the platform and caught Newman's arm. "Mr. Newman, please. You must address this crowd. Please, sir." His face wet, Mr. Joruchoff assisted Newman to the stage.

"Ladies and gentlemen, friends. This day could not have occurred without Jake Newman. He's the man from New York who never forgot his home town. He is a local fellow, and he is proud of this town. Jake helped bring us together, so that this march, this moment, could come to pass. I think of how lucky we are to have him with us."

Applause greeted Jake as he came to the platform. Throughout the crowd there was a feeling of quiet cheer, a sense of accomplishment, and, most of all, a feeling of peace.

"Thank you for allowing me to walk the streets of this town with you," Newman began. "I have always liked these tree-lined streets." Newman's words provoked a laugh from the crowd delighted with his presence.

"These streets contain your houses and your gardens. But mostly these streets are the places where people get to know one another. The streets are the by- ways of our society that tell us if our society works. The streets teach tolerance and the need we have for one other. The streets are for saying 'hello'. Our dreams navigate down such streets before they can be realized, before they become visible for others to see and to experience." Newman took a couple of deep breaths.

"The people who live in these tenements, shop in these stores, and go about their lives on these streets have much to teach us about hard work, family pride, and religious faith. By allowing your voices and your feet to support these people, you show that you understand that the streets belong to everyone.

When others forget this fact, they must be reminded. These forty miles have shown us that for every injustice there must be a human expression that sends out a message that violence and fear can never triumph.

That fateful evening, that Sunday when three streams of angry people plotted and participated in a march down this Square with sticks, and fists, and menacing intentions, those young men needed a reminder about citizenship and basic human understanding.

Somewhere along the way those fellows thought it was acceptable to try and intimidate people and that their actions were somehow patriotic and worthy of praise. Somewhere along the line those youths got the wrong message about how America works.

After their arraignment, it was argued that these youths were just playing a prank and their violence was misunderstood. It was argued that calling people the name 'dirty Jew' was, at most, unfortunate.

Unfortunate! The police called the youths 'marsh lads', fellows who were well-known to them and the community.

While no one has so far condoned what was done, some members of the community have minimized this riot. No one died. Thankfully, this is true. No one did die.

What if someone had died? Maybe then what happened there might have been called a riot. Some people may have called it a pogrom, which was Poland's and Russia's way of intimidating Jews by having some Jews beaten or killed by 'inflamed patriots'.

What if someone had died in Suffolk Square during that evening of rage? No, the marsh lads wanted to frighten the Jews, not kill anybody. It has been said the real culprit or source of anger in the town, the anger that these fellows represented, was over the lingering depression, and maybe the perception that some people are directly responsible for the economic collapse. Maybe Roosevelt's a Jew ... maybe he's a Jew lover. His wife is surely a Jew lover, and she loves Black people, too!

Well, folks, that is what this demonstration was all about. No people deserve that kind of message. People have rights, you know. But people around here and across this country have also got a sense of what is right. Sure, sometimes people get mixed up and take the wrong road, but this country is not going to support hate mongers, either disguised as marsh lads or Ku Kluxers.

Fortunately, no one died. It's unfortunate that an evening of fear happened at all. Unfortunate.

Every outrage is unfortunate, just as it was unfortunate that those citizens who witnessed the attack did little to prevent it from happening. Some of those people were looking outside their windows; some were police officers entrusted to serve the public, all of the public.

It was unfortunate that citizens ducked their heads and that children were told to hush and come in from the outdoors, or that their mothers and fathers turned their heads so they would not watch such a display.

It is unfortunate when religions preach against other religions. That is a mistake, a religious error, and an error in the way America operates. Praise to God there is religious freedom in America. But there is also a standard of ethics that yells foul when the Klan takes aim at the Catholics, or when Father Coughlin rants at the 'Jew Deal'. There is something ugly about that kind of talk. That talk is poison, the same kind of poison that is running rampant all over Europe today.

It is unfortunate when America sounds like a place going through a religious war, when religion is free and private and beyond anyone's bounds.

It is unfortunate, and it always will be unfortunate, that the Negro is a living reminder of how we succumbed to slavery and discrimination and one kind or another of continuing injustice. Yes, you know that is so.

It is unfortunate. But tell me ladies and gentlemen, tell me if you can when this unfortunate legacy will end.

Tell me my friends, which of you, who in our midst, who in this nation, will give us a hint when this unfortunate legacy will end.

It's unfortunate. Insults to humanity do not belong in this town, not here in America where we have more than enough to keep us busy working on a host of imperfections that shame us in the same breath as we declare ourselves a special land, a special society. Shame on us; unfortunate for us."

Newman did not want to but his eyes searched for Reverend Henson within the crowd. Newman saw him listening, just listening and patient the way a person waits for anything that is sane or right to reveal itself. America made people like Henson expect that their patience was a virtue, and Newman knew that to be an exaggeration. Patience was a veiled despair. Newman's words could not say what his heart believed, but Newman's eyes could not condone anything but this truth.

"Shame on us," Newman repeated.

"It is unfortunate. The courts may need time to catch up

to the threat that those forty-odd youths posed in these streets, but that is the way justice often proceeds. At least the courts worked. Maybe not to our satisfaction, but they did serve notice.

The courts worked but everyday justice, everyday vigilance, everyday ethics have not reached the heights that we value. We must say to ourselves that decency exists. People make a community work, and this community has not worked ... not until this day.

You worked together magnificently in these past hours. Something forty years in aimless pursuit of a just community could not realize, you realized in the rain and in the drizzle of this summer day.

Your feet and your hands rejected fear and violence and bore witness to a higher standard of conduct. Oh, you did not change the world. You did not end the sickness of hate either in our streets or in the streets where Nazi Brown Shirts prowl. But you made a statement that, even though faint in the scope of our world, was at the least a beginning, a voice that needed to be spoken.

Your message was clear. Your feet and your hours in this rain were in opposition to a life in which fear and unkindness sought to triumph, and this we rejected.

Thank you for your sacrifice and your courage and for being here."

Newman was applauded for expressing the feeling of the crowd. Fifty pairs of hands helped him down from the platform.

Then, the rains came in earnest, washing the streets clean of people and their umbrellas. The people knew that their job was done, and Newman was grateful that the demonstration lasted as long as it did.

Mr. Ginsburg and three other men moved the tables into the hotel lobby. The Square was now empty. In a matter of moments only the heavy pelting rain occupied the streets and air within the Square. Heavy torrents of water rolled past the gutters, making their way to storm drains and then disappearing to wherever rain descends.

Newman left, too. His sports jacket was soaked, and his shoes were as wet as his hair. In his room, he changed his clothes, took his suitcase down, and started packing his few belongings. His job was done. He sat down behind the Olivetti and typed out his final report.

****

Beckah's daughter, Sarah, was waiting in the lobby of the hotel when Newman went down to pay his final bill. She looked tired, and Newman was glad to see her. But there was another look on her face, too. It was a serious, painful kind of gaze.

"What you made this town go through turned out to be a good thing. Maybe even my father will see that someday. But my family paid the price for this. My father is upset, my mother ... she is a different person. You brought all this on, Mr. Newman. Are we the sacrificial lamb for your success?"

"Sarah, you helped make the march bring people together. Isn't that success? It is a kind of success, but that doesn't make me jump for joy. What I'm glad about is that we tried to let people know something - something about justice, something about what matters to us as a nation. This is our country, and it matters that we don't let it down. Sure, it is a Jewish thing, and it is an American thing. Just like its about young people and old people. It is all people. Everything about what happened here is just that - people. That is the only statement."

Sarah listened, but she had a message and that message was not to be frustrated. "But my family has suffered. My father and mother are at two different sides of the moon, and all I can do is watch. But I agree with my father. You brought all this on. You made this happen."

"I was little more than the messenger. This town can't

201

escape the kind of craziness taking place in the world. Listen, I've spent the greater part of my life looking for cover ... a place that was beyond the rat race. It doesn't exist."

Sarah seemed less the willowy young girl as she listened and as she spoke. "That's where I agree with my father. This is all going to pass, and we will just get on with our lives. You won't let this pass. He is right. You're dragging everybody into trouble."

"I've got to go."

"Go ahead, Mr. Newman. Go. My father says that is what you do best. Drift in and out of people's lives with nothing to lose. You've got nothing to lose, no life, no family ..."

"Take care, Sarah. Thanks for your help." Slowly, Newman walked up the staircase to his room.

****

Later, Newman and Mr. Ginsburg said goodbye. The two men shook hands and hugged one another.

"Mr. Newman, you will come back, won't you?" Mr. Ginsburg asked.

"Sure, of course I will. But I've got to get the same room," Newman joked but he knew that this would be his last time in the town.

"I guarantee it," Mr. Ginsburg laughed.

"This is my address in New York. You can reach me there," Newman said and handed him a card.

"Should I give this address to anyone in particular?" Mr. Ginsburg asked.

"Sure, give it to anyone, anyone in particular that you want. You decide, my friend. I have great faith in your judgment." Newman laughed and so did Ginsburg.

"You made me laugh, Mr. Newman. I shall miss that."

Back upstairs, a boy came to pick up Newman's bag.

"You're new here, aren't you? When I came here, I had to carry my own bag."

"Yes, I am, sir."

"What's your name?"

"Jackie Forbes. I live a few streets over on Rich Street."

"I remember the street and even that name. I used to know a Raymond Forbes."

"That was my father. He died about a year ago."

"He was a nice fellow. You look like him." Newman handed him a dollar bill, and the boy looked shocked. "Thank you, sir," he blurted out.

"Send these to the train for me." Newman walked down the stairs, and he admired the scale of the stairs and the railings and how New England possessed a fine sense of proportion that was reflected in everything from the chairs and stairs and all throughout such buildings.

CONCLUSION

The summer had so parched the earth that even a hard rainfall had hardly loosened the ground. Newman looked out the window of his compartment as the train crawled from Boston's South Station. He had positioned his large suitcase on the seat opposite him, hoping to discourage any traveler from joining him. He wanted to enjoy the passing scenery. He was in no rush to get into New York City, and he even toyed with the idea of getting off the train in a little town somewhere, anywhere, along the way. Such a fantasy was part of a lifelong game he played wondering how he would adjust to an anonymous place, how he would act as an anonymous person.

"What a fantasy," he thought. "Can you imagine yourself in Montàna? Why not? Is it because a Jew cannot live by himself and still be a Jew? That a Jew needs other Jews? Is that your reason?" Newman questioned himself.

"Maybe it is. Maybe it's the reason that that little town - the one that just trickled by - can't shelter me. Oh, give the town a break! You aren't ready for it. That's the truth. You just aren't ready for any place." And Newman left it at that. Gone was even the wistful notion of a tiny house lodged within a large moor.

His destiny decided, Newman opened his carry-on. From inside, he pulled out the manilla envelope that contained Jenny's writings. Leafing through the material, he was thankful that Beckah had included the poems, letters, a diary, and songs. He looked forward to reading everything he had in the envelope. Whatever had been on Jenny's mind mattered to him just as everything in Jenny's life seemed a part of his.

He began with the diary that Jenny had kept for nearly three years. The entries began on the first of January 1939, and stopped four months before her death.

December 22, 1939

We went around the room today talking about Chanukah. The children are hoping for gifts so that they will not feel envious of their Christian friends on Christmas Day. Almost every child has a cold or a virus, but we enjoy our time together. I hope to make some Chanukah gifts for them. Anything that needs to be unwrapped lights up their faces.

February 24, 1940

This is such an elitist place, but especially this year when the students fall into two categories: those who can afford it and those who cannot.

There are a handful of Jewish students. Professor S. in the Humanities Department was complaining about "the settlement house" atmosphere at the school. I asked him what he meant by this. "Well, the college does have an historic constituency, the kind of people one needs to look to in hard times."

There is such a mean-spirited quality to Prof. S. He is so haughty that it's no surprise the students detest him, even those of the "historic constituency". Such a wasted person. His vitae boasts his Harvard B.A. and his Yale M.A. and Ph.D., but he is such a fraud. Not a sentence has ever flowed from his mouth that is not ripened by some form of reaction.

****

The diaries were testimony to Jenny's disenchantment with the academic world. It was not only that the people were full of intellectual snobbery and pretext, but that there was something mean-spirited about the exclusiveness of the ivory tower, about the elitism that diminished the humanity of those who lived beyond the iron-grated fence that surrounded the campus.

Jenny grew cynical about the college's social commitments and even its intellectual credibility. That stamp of a college's approval, the diploma which drove her to such a frenzy, was seen by her as a house of cards. She saw herself as a fool, believing in the mission of knowledge but aghast at the puny individuals who advanced the cause.

Jake continued to read from the February entries.

February 28, 1940

"I am ashamed of myself. It is hard for me to know what motivated me. Was it ambition? Was that my sin? That is poetic justice. It appears that now I have no ambition, and all that remains is a sense of my sin."

Jake realized that Jenny had discovered how used she

had been, even used by herself. While she spent her time behind the librarian's desk, knowledgeable about so many subjects, no one seemed to notice or care. No one even bothered to ask her her opinion or a question.

In her poems and in her lyrics, she expressed her fate, her errors, her misjudgments, her sadness in having her faith come crashing down upon her.

It was clear that the war in Europe and the horror of anti-Semitism affected her. Her diary was filled with bits and pieces of newspaper reports of Nazi provocations and intimidations.

"Life is even less than cheap, and the world is less than concerned" was her diary entry on the last day of 1940.

Then Jake read one of Jenny's poems that was written on a single piece of paper, folded as though it were stuffed in a pocket or a pocketbook. Newman had difficulty getting this poem out of his mind. The poem had no title and no date.

> Inside every Jew there is a poor Jew,
> a tattered and weary spirit,
> (maybe only a tiny part of a person),
> who realizes the illusion of well being.
> A person whose memory spans five thousand
> years of Jewish life,
> with a memory steeped
> in recrimination and
> lesson upon lesson of a failed humanity.

> Inside every Jew there is a
> potential Jew,
> that individual whose living
> is ground upon a tradition,
> bound up
> within the spirit of the world,
> alive, a God-given world,

a world that must be returned
to God.

Inside every Jew, there is the
dust of the road just ahead.
There will be a tomorrow
where every man and woman and child
has a right to
the road,
to a tomorrow in a
world of hope,
a world of remembrance.
That is the Jew,
the inhabiter of the world,
the one
in search of living,
in memory of every generation.

Newman stopped reading. It had grown dark.

****

With his lap full of papers, Newman dozed. The train helped him sleep. He had grown accustomed to its mild jostling of his body. His eyes opened to see his hands holding Jenny's papers. The feel of his hands returned. He wanted to read. He randomly chose an entry.

April 11, 1937

I think I understand what the golden calf symbolized. God does not take it lightly when the Chosen People worship some other god - even a god made of gold. Don't we see ourselves as a speck of gold? Aren't we admirers of our minds and our accomplishments? Something of the golden calf is in each of us. I know there is a piece of that creature within me, and I get angry with myself when I bow before that beast.

The golden calf speaks the language of making choices. Choices! What is celebrated is not our destiny but the choices we've made! No wonder that I so despise the house of cards I've built. My choices!

****

"It's about time that you got back to that desk." The Director's voice was strident and hoarse.

"Literally, I just got here. I take it you missed me?" Newman joked and stretched out his hand.

"Well, I knew you'd be doing your job, whatever it might actually be, but someone else was looking for you. She's in my office now."

Newman looked at the Director and quickly headed to his office. He opened the door to a "Hello, Jake."

Beckah's face was lit by the sun from a window that had neither curtains nor a shade. The Director's cat was nestled in her lap, asleep. She placed her hands underneath the cat's sleeping body and gently rested her on the chair. She stood.

"I had to come, Jake."

"I'm glad you did." As he reached out to touch her, his arms embraced her, and he kissed her. She returned his kiss. Once in each other's arms, everything in their lives made sense. There was a peace that each brought to the other.

"I love you." Newman's lips mouthed the words that made him realize how buried his life had been.

Beckah looked directly at him. "The first time we met, my heart began to beat. You made my heart come alive."

****

The long and extraordinarily thin cat meandered out of the Director's office and followed a path that led to Newman's desk where the Director now sat staring out a distant window. The cat leaped onto the director's lap sniffing at his hands, waiting for familiar, gentle strokes.

"You are a pretty girl, my little friend, but you know that, don't you? Were you sent packing from my office by those two? I bet you were. You will have to forgive them. Those two people didn't know you were there. They were happy to find one another. One of the better accidents of life - to find someone. They meant you no slight. Sit here on my lap."

The cat nestled its way into a comfortable position, enjoying the patting of her head, the gentle fingering of her pointed ears, and the serenity of the moment.

"Yes, pretty one. Just sit here. You and I, one old cat and one old man." And the Director laughed. Though there were people in the office moving from one desk to the next, carrying on their duties, the Director sat as though unseen.

"My little friend. Yes, you are my little friend. You are more than that, but you know that. Shall we go in that office and disturb those people? Huh?"

But the cat lying with its tail surrounding her body rested.

"Ah, you are right, my little friend. It is time to rest. When you are an old man, it is time to rest." The Director stroked the cat with a single finger, not wanting to disturb her sleep. "Rest. Rest."

And the Director did not utter another word.

EPILOGUE

Goodbye, Again

I don't remember what it was I cried for,
must have been things I just don't need
and never did.
Fancy dresses and diamond rings,
all those things
people say they love.

Sad little lies, that is all that survives,
All that survives and then goodbye.
And love, has that been my disguise,
a disguise so that I might hide,
love, one of my little lies?

Love, would I really know you?

I don't remember what it was I wanted,
I don't recall what was special about my life,
All I know is that something happened,
summer houses and evening dresses,
forgetful friends and fast romances.

Sad little lies, that is all that survives,
All that survives and then goodbye.
And love, have you been my disguise,
Love, one of my little lies.

There is a world I must come to know,
A place where sun and rain and snow
Makes me want to know,
Is this the world to love,
Can this be a world of love?

Fancy dresses and diamond rings,
all the things people say they love.
Sad little lies, that is all that survives,
All that survives and then goodbye.

Maybe love can make it right.
Love, would I really know you?

Goodbye again, goodbye to all those things
I've longed for,
Goodbye to dreams that now make me laugh,
goodbye to everybody else's pain.

Love, a special love, may it come to me fast.

Sad little lies, that is all that survives,
All that survives and then goodbye.
All that survives and then goodbye.

****